# H THE ackers

## OF Oz

## by Tom Mula

## Illustrations by Jason Fuller

dog ear
PUBLISHING

Published by
Dog Ear Publishing
4010 W. 86th Street, Ste H
Indianapolis, IN 46268
www.dogearpublishing.net

ISBN: 978-1-4575-1564-4 (Paperback Edition)
ISBN: 978-1-4575-1562-0 (Hardcover Edition)
This book is printed on acid-free paper.

*With love and thanks to*
*L. Frank Baum*
*for bringing so much*
*light and laughter*
*into our world*

*This book is dedicated*
*to Margaret Hamilton*

## PROLOGUE

… a sound, like tapping on a window, and a muffled voice: "Kid! Hey! Hey, kid!"

## CHAPTER ONE

# An Innocent Village Far Away

"She's coming."

Stainless steel, harsh fluorescents. A long steel table, backed by a bank of brushed-steel freezers, refrigerators, ranges, and frosted-glass cabinets.

Tight-lipped whispers. Several well-dressed young men, gray sharkskin suits, perfect haircuts, pants a little too tight, huddle together, shuffling stainless-steel clipboards. Foreheads get wiped. Upper lips get blotted. Expensive watches get checked.

In the corner, one of them is barfing quietly into a plastic baggie from the supply room.

"She's coming? How can you tell?"

"Jervé always gets sick just before—"

The brushed-steel doors at the far end of the studio slide open, an oily, expensive sound. The yapping of lots of yappy little white dogs as She sweeps in—a beautiful entrance, of course. Flowing chiffon gowns, wings of perfect auburn hair, perfect makeup, perfect smile—

*Perfect Lady*. That's the name of the show, *Perfect Lady*, beamed daily to 20 million adoring, slavish imitators in more than a dozen time zones. It's called *Perfect Lady*, but you might as well call it *Don't Bother to Try, It's a Lost Cause; Really, It's Sweet, But Seriously, the Best You Can Do is only ALMOST as Good as Me.*

"Cameron, kiss kiss, hold the mutts for me, will you?" as She hands one of the young men half a dozen leashes. "Is everything ready, oh my, the set looks fabulous, perfect, as always—" that wonderful, smoky, baritone voice, a cross between some old-time wire-hanger movie star and "Luke, I am your father"—

"Is this my mark, everybody ready, how's my hair, boys—"

A chorus: "Perfect, Miss Van Lear."

The yappy little white dogs are still yapping. Her voice, like a crowbar: "*Shut it, rodents.*"

Five of them sit instantly, instantly silent.

She looks at the one still yapping. "*Sheldon, I said shut it.*" He does.

At the name Sheldon, all of the well-dressed young men shudder, and the room gets a whole lot colder. Tiny waterfalls of perspiration creep from under their perfect haircuts. Jervé starts throwing up again, but silently, because the tape is rolling... "5, 4, —, —, —"

"Good afternoon, and welcome to *Perfect Lady*. Today, we're all about *succulents*." She puts on her potting apron, the one with the darling ruffles and the adorable pewter broomstick pinned over where her heart would be if she had one.

2

"We're going to begin by repotting a *Sclumbergia Zygocactus* (which you might know as the Christmas Cactus). Now, when you're re-potting spiny cacti (which should be done yearly) a good way of handling them to keep from getting 'pricked—'" (a mischievous look to the camera) "—is to wrap the cactus first in a little bit of bubble-wrap, securing it with a twist tie, or just a plain old rubber... CUT!"

Naked fear. For a moment, only silence. "Is there something the matter, Miss Van Lear?"

"No, there's nothing the matter," She smiles sweetly, "if you're trying to kill the poor little thing. Look at this. Come here. Come here, look at it."

The well-dressed young man with the biggest clipboard steps closer. He is drenched, sweating freely now, frowning at the table, trying desperately to guess what's wrong. After a moment, a tentative shot-in-the-dark: "Aha."

"I knew you'd see it! Now, just tell everyone here what's wrong."

"Well, the, um, the... uhhh—"

"Exactly. I asked for *sandy* soil, and what is this? I ask you, *what is this?*"

"Well, it's not exactly, uh—"

"This is *compost*! Compost! For a succulent! You're going to give this poor little cactus *mealy bugs*! Is that what you want?"

"I'm sorry, Miss Van Lear, we'll take care of it right—"

"Whose fault is this?" No answer. "Who brought

me compost when I asked for a peat mix with a 60-percent grit?" No answer. "I'm waiting."

Nothing, only the sound of well-dressed young men perspiring, and the click of perfect fingernails on stainless steel.

"You know how I get when I have to wait."

Once again, the sound of Jervé barfing quietly in the corner. She turns.

"Jervé? Jervé, dear, are you ill?"

"No, Miss Van—hllp. Hllp."

"Jervé, come here, please. Is this the soil I asked you for?"

"No, Miss V—hllp."

"I asked for what, Jervé?"

"A peat mix with a 60-percent—hllp, hllp, hllp."

"And this isn't it, is it?"

"No, ma'am. Hllp."

"Well, while—" She looks at the well-dressed young man with the largest clipboard. "What's your name, dear?"

"Kyle, Miss Van—"

"Kyle? Really, Kyle?"

"Yes, ma'am."

"Lovely name. Masculine. Understated. I like it." She turns to the group. "From now on, you're *all* Kyle. Well, while Kyle here is getting the *correct* soil, the soil I *asked* for, Jervé, why don't you step into my office for a moment?"

Jervé looks to the Kyles for rescue, help, a word, anything. All he sees are the tops of heads, perfect haircuts studying shoes, nails, clipboards.

Sweating and hllp-ing, he follows her.

The click, click, click of perfect heels on the perfectly polished marble floor. The sound of the massive door to her office as it shuts: hardly a sound at all, more the movement of something huge in the air, like the sound of earth swallowing an innocent village far away. Well-dressed young men scurry, making the necessary changes in silence, each straining to listen to the sounds not coming from the office. There are no raised voices. No pleading. No laughter, no cries. After a while, they all just stand there, for hours, it seems, listening and staring at the door.

Which finally opens.

To yapping.

They all hear it, the yapping coming from inside the office.

And She sweeps in, all smiles, leading another yapping dog, another little white dog on a leash, yapping behind her. She leads him over to one of the Kyles—

"Kyle, be a dear and hold on to Jervé for me, won't you?"

Shudders. They start shooting again.

*She* turns to the camera.

Her smile is just perfect.

## CHAPTER TWO

# The Smell of Dried Flowers

Elizabeth was prepared. She handed her mother the bunch of sage they'd paid too much for on their last trip to Sedona. "Careful, Mom, this sage is pretty dry."

It was sunrise, their first morning in the new house. Rose was wearing the tie-dyed purple thing she always wore when she did this new-agey stuff. Her shock of ginger hair was tied back with some feathers, and she'd glued a teardrop-shaped purple rhinestone between her eyebrows with eyelash adhesive. On the coffee table in front of her were some crystals, a bell, and a lit candle. She reached the sage towards the candle. "Don't you worry, Bets, your mom is an old hand at this—"

"Be careful, mom, it's really very—" Rose touched the sage to the candle. It exploded.

Elizabeth's mother was suddenly dancing around holding a ball of flame the size of her head. "Ooh, ooh, ooh, honey, get the—"

Elizabeth picked up the fire extinguisher, and

pressed the trigger. Rose disappeared in a noisy cloud of $CO_2$ as Elizabeth gassed her mom.

This had happened before. Elizabeth was prepared.

"Nice going, Bets." Her mother's face was black now, except for two white cartoon rings around her eyes. "Guess we can skip the sage, huh?"

Rose rang the bell, and circled the coffee table three times. "You'll see, honey—Barrington is going to be a wonderful place for us. The schools here are great, it's really close to the Chicago..."

"Sure, mom."

"And fourth grade is going to be different, you'll see. Even though you're starting a little late, you're going to make lots of friends here." She rang the bell again, and sprinkled water into the four corners of the room.

"And this new job—sweetie, this new job is going to make things so much better for both of us—"

She threw kosher salt liberally around her.

Elizabeth sighed. She knew who was going to have to clean that up.

"Stop sighing, dear, this is the important part." She stood up straighter and addressed the air. "Bless this house with peace and love and joy and light—may all who dwell here, and all who enter, be blessed."

Then she held out her hands. "Beings of light, I invite thee, I invite thee, I invite thee. Come and be welcome."

The world held its breath, and for a second, Rose's words hung in the air like the vibration of a great crystal bell. Elizabeth raised her eyebrows. "That was nice, mom. New. Where did that come from?"

"Who knows? Just came to me, sperm of the moment." Rose made her I-just-made-a-joke face and blew out the candle. She looked up at the scorched spot on the ceiling. "I'm sure a little Fantastik will clean that right up," and she left the room to change.

Elizabeth unfolded the ladder, and picked up the Fantastik, the scrubby sponge, and the paper towels.

She already had them. Elizabeth was *prepared*.

Elizabeth was a knobby little girl, knobby elbows, knobby knees sticking out of cargo shorts, braces, big shoes, big glasses. She had her mom's ginger hair, tied out of the way into two pony tails. She had her mom's big blue eyes, too, swimming behind her glasses like two goldfish in a bowl. No one ever said that Elizabeth was pretty. Often they said something like,

"What a *smart* little girl." "What a *bright* little girl." "Ingenious." "Efficient." "Prepared." They also often used words like "control freak" or "annoying." Elizabeth was okay with this.

Because there was nothing wrong with Elizabeth. She just knew how things should be. "I know how things should be. Why don't people listen?" she would say. But, generally, people don't want someone else telling them how things should be, especially if they're right. And ten. And Elizabeth was often right.

So at school, Elizabeth often ate lunch by herself.

Elizabeth was okay with this.

But, scrubbing at the scorch on the ceiling, Elizabeth wondered why she *wasn't* okay. Usually, the start of the new school year was one of the best times in the world: *time for new school supplies*. New pencils and new notebooks. A new backpack. And a stapler. And scissors, paper clips, rubber bands, several colors of markers, a stopwatch, Kleenex, a three-hole punch, Scotch tape, duct tape, and Band-Aids.

A whistle.

A mirror for signaling.

Perhaps a compass.

Usually, the afternoon they had spent at the office-supply store would have made her happy for weeks. But instead, this whole thing—the move, the boxes, the dusty dead fly on the fake-wood-grained windowsill—made her feel… empty. Unsettled.

*Lonely.*

The day before they'd left Minnesota, Elizabeth had walked around touching everything, saying goodbye to the birch-and-cedar woods she'd played pirates in, saying goodbye to the field still peppered with wildflowers at the beginning of October, saying goodbye to the butterfly tree, the working farm where she'd learned to drive a pickup sitting on her mother's lap. Their new house was the smallest, cheapest house in snooty-suburban Barrington, quite a change from the hundred-year-old family farmhouse. Elizabeth had sighed when she saw the worn fake-wood floors, the prickly, pointy, white-painted walls, the hollow fake-wood door on her closet that had already slid off its rollers.

But Elizabeth couldn't complain. The weight of Guilt pressed down on her knobby little shoulders.

This was all her fault.

They'd moved here because of her.


A few months before, Elizabeth had been having a terrible day.

The saddest words in the world are, "What party?"

Elizabeth said them at 12:17 around a mouthful of PBJ, sitting on the bleachers during first-period lunch.

She was sitting by herself, of course, but she overheard Francy Linardi and Brandy Timmerman talking really loudly behind her, loud enough for Elizabeth to hear every word, talking at great length about how much *fun* it had been.

The day got worse. Just after two, Heather Osborne-

Mott, whose party it had been, came up to her and said, "Geek-squ—, I mean Betsy, could you give me a hand? (gum-pop, gum-pop, blinding white teeth flash, toss of golden locks). I don't know why this file won't open, it's my homework for Comp-blab, I *probably* saved it (gum-pop) but I don't know, can you do *anything*?" Heather Osborne-Mott had shampoo-commercial hair and was the only girl in third grade at Ronald Reagan Shining Light whose mother let her wear nail polish every day. Today, the color was "Jungle Red." Next to her, Elizabeth felt like a small, brown, warty toad.

'Geek-squad,' eh? thought Elizabeth. 'Party last weekend,' eh? 'Bwah-hah-hah-hah, revenge is mine,' said the cartoon-devil-voice in her head. Elizabeth felt the devil-horns sprouting, and her fingers itched for Heather's keyboard. "Why, certainly, Heather, it would be my pleasure, nothing would please me more than to be of assistance, let me just tap into your class file…" She wouldn't actually blue-screen her, but with a few taps of the keyboard, well, *many* things were possible. Elizabeth was the best programmer at R.R.S.L.; she'd taught some of the teachers how to use the programs that came with the new computer-lab, and as a result, she had everybody's passwords.

The Hacker's Code flashed through Elizabeth's head: "Are you a White Hat or a Black Hat?" Elizabeth ignored it and crammed the black hat down around her ears. With a few taps of the keyboard, she arranged for a couple of gross of big-butt granny-panties and a case of Slimfast to be special-delivered to Heather at the beginning of gym class; not this afternoon, in a month or so, plenty of time to be innocently somewhere else when sweet, sweet revenge shook down.

"Glad to help, anytime," Elizabeth said, but as she watched Heather flounce off (gum-pop, giggle, slow-motion vanishing into a ray of sunshine), she knew that she didn't really feel any better, and that what she'd just done had made her even more itchy and irritated. Grrr.

Elizabeth sighed; she was glad the day was almost over. As she reached into her pocket for a pencil, she discovered that her hand was moist. She looked down. One of her highlighters had opened up and there was a big yellow stain on her brand new cargo shorts that smelled like ammonia and looked like, well, pee.

Elizabeth wondered how long that had been there. Then she remembered how, *happy* everyone had been to see her all day. All day long everyone, especially Heather, had talked to her with big, big smiles. The stain had probably been there for a while.

So at the end of the day, when Elizabeth, with her jacket tied around her waist, was standing on the sidewalk next to Tony Cervanka, the dreamy new fourth-grader from Springfield who had just moved there a month ago, when her crazy mom pulled up in her rock band's twenty-year-old conversion van with the picture of cats wearing eye-patches and "The Pussy Pirates" semi-professionally spray-painted on the side, Elizabeth tried really hard to disappear.

Too late. "Betsy! Hooo-ooo! Here I am!"

Elizabeth tried even harder to become invisible as

her mom hung out the van window and waved. She'd had a gig that afternoon, and was still wearing her pirate outfit: bandana, dreadlocks, eyepatch, parrot. "Arrrr! Avast, girly! Ye'd best be gettin' your wee heinie in here!"

Tony Cervanka grinned. "Your mom? Cool ride." He turned to the other fourth-grade boys lounging against the bike rack beside him. "Hey guys, look at Geek Squad's awesome wheels!"

Elizabeth felt the edges of her ears flame and turn scarlet. She thought things couldn't get any worse, but then her mom yelled, "Betsy Gale Callahan, get your rear in gear!" and leaned on the horn.

The band-van blasted "La Cucaracha."

Two verses.

Elizabeth's face blazed like a wildfire. She hoisted her backpack to her shoulder, stomped to the van, and slammed the door, hard. She slammed the door at the fourth-grade boys now singing and dancing in a conga line, slammed the door at this stupid airbrushed band-van, slammed the door at this stupid school, this stupid pee stain, this stupid party she hadn't been invited to, and most of all, slammed the door at herself for *caring* about this stupid, stupid—

"Sorry about the band-van, Bets, but the pickup threw a rod."

And of course, Elizabeth struck out at the only person in the world who only, only loved her, and she said the words that changed everything:

"Why couldn't *I* have a *normal* mom?"

Silence.

*Silence.*

Crickets. Tumbleweeds. The sound of the wind whistling across the Minnesota prairie.

Elizabeth couldn't look. She didn't have to. She knew how hard Rose worked to make a life for both of them. She knew how sensitive her crazy mom was, how much her mom adored her. Elizabeth knew that if she looked at Rose then, her mother's lip would be trembling. Elizabeth couldn't bear that. So instead of looking, she pretended she hadn't said anything, and rode all the way home making hilarious jokes about her school day that they both pretended to laugh at. That night, Elizabeth cooked Rose's favorite dinner, cheesy-brown-rice-and-broccoli.

But the seed of destruction had been planted; the damage had been done. Elizabeth's mom was unusually quiet for the whole weekend. All weekend, every time Elizabeth rounded a corner, her mom would be staring out the window with a cold cup of coffee in her hand, or watching TV with the sound turned off.

Then Rose got busy. There was a blizzard of activity and she spent late nights on the Internet doing research and sending out letters and résumés, and doing interviews on Skype. For months nothing happened, depressed economy, lots of people looking for work. Although Rose looked glummer and glummer, Elizabeth heaved a secret sigh of relief. Dodged that bullet. Whew.

Then, one Sunday night around the Fourth of July, cicadas humming and the sweet smell of corn-pollen in the air, as Elizabeth finished the after-supper dishes, she heard a squeal from her mother's bedroom — "Wha-hooooo!!!" Rose came dancing into the kitchen waving a printout, "Pardner, we're in business!"

She picked Elizabeth up, and danced her around the kitchen, singing, "Guess who's got a big-deal job-offer, guess, you'll never guess! Yuppiedom, here we come!"

"What happened, mom?"

"I don't know, some kind of miracle! I'd just about given up, when out of nowhere, for no reason, it's CRAZY! Really, a huge surprise, makes absolutely NO sense, this BIG company in Chicago noticed my résumé online, and hired me, just like that! Miraculous, really! Like winning the lottery or something! Really, just crazy, insane, crazy luck! Out of the blue! Total surprise. Kind of spooky, really. Weird."

Elizabeth felt a chill then, and the phrase "like someone had walked over her grave" skittered through her mind. She felt the hairs on her arms stand up.

But she laughed along with Rose, and made her this-is-terrific-mom face to be supportive and all, but in her heart she felt like there was a tidal wave building above their heads. She wanted to say, hold on, let's think a minute, but suddenly things were moving very fast and everything had changed. By September, the farm had been sold.

Now it was the second week of October, and they were in Barrington.

Here they were, in the smallest house in Barrington, with hollow, fake-wood doors and prickly white-plaster walls and a dead fly on the windowsill, a house that was full of cardboard boxes. Gone was the farm, gone were the meadows, gone were the woods and streams and secret places Elizabeth had played in for the first nine years of her life.

But Elizabeth couldn't complain.

It was her fault they were here.

They had moved here because of her.


"Pretty good, girlfriend. Looks like the paint was hardly burned at all. Pancakes for breakfast?" Her mom had scrubbed her face and changed. Even in a tee-shirt and jeans, she looked terrific.

Elizabeth and her mom were different. Rose Callahan had been a great beauty in her time, and she still turned heads when they went to the mall. Rose had this amazing tumbleweed of ginger-colored hair, and the kind of blue eyes that made long-distance truck-drivers stand in front of her stammering and digging their toes into the floor. She'd had a lot of interesting boyfriends—a sculptor, a gourmet chef, a guy who'd taught Elizabeth how to sail, poets and bartenders and construction workers. Rose'd had many interesting careers, too: She'd been an actress, been a dancer, sung lead in front of some pretty terrible rock bands. You could call her spacey, flighty, scattered, unfocused, short-attention-span, ADD. But you could never call her boring. Or bored.

The only things Elizabeth and her mother shared,

really, were their eyes and that shock of ginger-colored hair. Rose was the dreamer who put things off. Elizabeth was the one who paid the bills on time, and made sure the library books were returned before they'd left Minnesota and that the Internet would be working when they moved in. Elizabeth cleaned up messes, Elizabeth made lists. Elizabeth was the one who worried.

"Betsy, honey, don't *fret*," her mom would say, as she rubbed the wrinkle between Elizabeth's eyebrows. Then she'd look at the ceiling and ask, "How did I get such an *old* little girl?"

After pancakes, Elizabeth stood in her bedroom. The bed hadn't been set up yet, and was leaning in pieces against the wall; connecting the computer had been the first priority. Now Elizabeth poked a toe at one of the boxes on the floor. Well-p, might as well get started. They weren't going to unpack themselves.

Suddenly there was a noise. It was coming from one of the boxes.

There was an old black trunk with brass corners and a hundred labels from all over the country at the bottom of the pile. Something inside it was *scratching*...

Elizabeth stood stock still, listening—had they moved a varmint here from Minnesota? It sounded bigger than a mouse, and *insistent*. Scratchy-scratchy-scratch.

Elizabeth picked up a broom. She crept up on the trunk, hoping that it wasn't a raccoon—they looked cute, but they could be nasty. Or a possum—even worse.

Ugh. Giant rats, all teeth and claws. Ugliest animals on the planet, possums. Scratchy-scratchy-scratch.

Elizabeth whacked the top of the trunk with the broom. That stopped it. For a few heart-thumping seconds, there was no noise. Then scratchy-scratchy-scratch, again. Elizabeth crept closer. She really, really didn't want something with teeth and claws jumping out at her. So she slowly, carefully, silently undid the trunk's brass clasps, and inched open the lid the barest amount, just a quarter of an inch.

Nothing.

An inch. Nothing. Nothing with claws or teeth so far.

Another inch. Still nothing. Standing as far away as possible, Elizabeth used the broom handle to give the lid a shove. The lid fell back with a creak and a dusty sigh, and a flower-smell rose from inside the trunk.

Elizabeth waited. Still nothing. She inched a few inches closer and poked around with the broom handle, pushing things aside and looking under things. Weird— there was nothing there, nothing that could have made the noise. There were only some old boxes, some old books, but at the bottom of the trunk was—

"Mom, what's this?"

"What's what, honey?"

"I found—" she carried the box into the room that would be her mother's bedroom if it ever got unpacked, "—I found this—"

Rose turned around and froze for a moment. Then she tilted her head to the side, and smiled a little smile.

"Oh, I'd forgotten about… C'mere, pardner." She put the box on the bed, inviting Elizabeth to sit beside her, and took off the lid. Inside the box was an ivory satin wedding dress, lovely and old, not yellowed, but golden, rich and buttery, with a veil decorated with dried poppies, packed in tissue and lovingly, perfectly preserved.

"That was Grammy Dot's dear. My grand—your great-grandmother's. I never got a chance to wear it. I was saving it for you." Her mother smoothed the veil, the lace, the satin, looking at the dress for a moment, with a lost expression, her mind somewhere else…

Elizabeth kept quiet. There was a story here, and sometimes if she kept her mouth shut, her mother might—

"I wish you could have known her. Grammy Dot."

"I thought maybe the dress was yours."

"Darling, you know there was never a man that was good enough for you. Although there was that time when Bruce Willis, after *Moonlighting* but before all the *Die Hard* movies…"

Elizabeth sighed. She'd never gotten a straight answer, and she was hoping that this might be the time. Her mom had told her lots of stories about who her dad was—an evening with Sting on a rock tour; an audition to play Ophelia with the most famous Hamlet of the '90s; the time she had interned at the White House. Her mom told great stories, and Elizabeth loved them all. But she had Google, so she'd done her own detective work, counting the nine months back from her birthday. This took her to the time her mom was studying dance with the New York City Ballet. Elizabeth wondered if there were more straight guys in the *corps de ballet* than people thought…

But she always loved the stories.

"Your Grammy Dot was one of those frontier women, she was—resilient. Do you know what that means, Bets? She was strong. She was like a willow sapling—you could bend her all the way to the ground, and as soon as you let go, she'd spring right back. She refused to be broken."

Her mother smoothed the dress in her lap. "I always hoped you would be like her. Resilient." A shadow crossed her mother's eyes, like a cloud-shadow rippling across a field. "I'm… not."

Elizabeth wondered what that shadow behind her mother's eyes was. Suddenly, she really loved her hippy-dippy mom, and she wished there was a way to make her feel better, to let her know how she felt. She wanted to rub away that wrinkle between her mom's eyebrows…

But she was only ten. A hug would have to do.

Rose shook a couple of tears from her eyes, and hugged her back. "Hey—look what I found! Girlfriend, you will be glad to know that I did *not* forget to pack the Official Pussy Pirates Eye-Patch!"

*"Left a good job in the city, working for the man down in New Orleans…"*

Elizabeth clapped along as her mom belted "Proud Mary" into a hairbrush, standing on top of the mattress, surrounded by piles of clothes and unopened boxes.

On the bed beside her was the box from the trunk: the old wedding dress, the veil, the poppies, and the silver shoes.

## CHAPTER THREE

# Weird Dreams

Everybody was having weird dreams that night:

A sound, like tapping on a window, and a muffled voice: "Kid! Hey! Hey kid!"

Tap, tap, tap, dull padded thuds, as if the hands wore mittens.

Elizabeth pulled a pillow over her head and went back to sleep.

Elsewhere, someone else was having this dream:

A gray vision of the gray street, *her* street, 7:45 on a sunless Monday morning, lightless stone canyons crowded with men and women in sober, respectable gray, cardboard cups in hand, running shoes, hurrying to their jobs, faces already tense and drawn—as they get closer, they file into neat lines, lines of worker-bees in gray, lockstep-marching into her building.

It's a good dream. She smiles.

And then, into this colorless world, in the distance, tiny, a dot of color, growing larger—above their heads, a patchwork flash in the distance, and the sound of— trumpets blaring over a loudspeaker, blaring what, a cha-cha? Fountains of paper fill the air—

She wakes up, sweating, turns on the light, lights a cigarette with a perfectly manicured hand, and draws deep. The perfectly manicured hand is shaking.

Elizabeth dreams another dream:

Naked. She was naked.

First day in a new school, getting on the school bus, naked.

Elizabeth said to herself, this is a perfectly pre-dictable projection of natural first-day-of-school anxiety. So she swung her book bag to her shoulder and sat down ignoring the laughter and applause, and hoping the dream would end soon and she could get dressed. Even though it was just the middle of October, the vinyl bus seat was like ice. It could have been worse. It could have been December.

Then the bus darkened, like it was going through a tunnel, or as if black clouds had suddenly clotted over the sun. Elizabeth was now alone on the bus—almost. She felt someone staring at the back of her neck. Even though she knew she wasn't going to like what she would see, she turned around to look.

The boy on the back seat was the color of a maggot; his skin was shiny and damp-looking like old deli meat.

His eyes were white, no pupils, only a dead-looking white like hard-boiled eggs. His head ticked back and forth like there was no mind there, only the song on his iPod. He looked at Elizabeth and smiled.

Worms spilled out from between his teeth. They dripped down onto his neat gray sport coat, spilling onto the seat and dropping to the floor with wet glops. The worms started to cover the floor of the bus, dead white and moving, tumbling towards her in a gloppy wave as the bus tilted and yawed crazily now, throwing Elizabeth back and forth, tumbling rolling waves of worms towards her.

Elizabeth knew what to do with scary dreams, her mom had taught her: Turn around and face what you fear, and, if you can, make friends with it. She walked down the aisle—wearing clothes again, thanks—towards the boy. She felt the worms squishing under her feet and sticking to her ankles, but she made her way to the back of the bus.

Hi, my name's Elizabeth, she said, and held out her hand.

The boy smiled up at her, white-eyed like something out of a zombie movie, then the bus pitched again, throwing Elizabeth onto him. There were no bones, he was just soft like a rotten banana, sticking to her hands, and she sank into him, wormy softness sucking at her, pulling her face into—

Elizabeth jolted herself upright, heart pounding, awake and shaking. As she fought to catch her breath, fought to calm herself down, she heard the other sound again: padded thuds like someone thumping on a window: "Kid! Hey kid!"

"Is anything the matter, hon? I heard you calling." Her door opened and her mom was standing there in the sweatclothes she always slept in. Elizabeth pulled the covers close. The room was freezing—no, she was drenched in sweat.

"Are you okay, honey?"

Elizabeth sat up in her sleeping bag, knuckling her eyes, blinking against the light. "Yeah, mom, I just had a bad dream, I'm fine."

"C'mon, let's have some chocolate—I'll heat up some milk. I had a bad dream, too. Looks like we could both use something with a shot in it."

Elizabeth put on her robe, and the two of them padded down to the kitchen in their slippers. "You too, huh?" said Elizabeth.

"Yes, and I won't tell you mine if you won't tell me yours."

"Probably just first-day jitters, both of us. New house, new school, new job, new bedroom…"

Rose took the old cast-iron pot out of a box on the floor, the pot she always used for hot milk. Elizabeth sat on a stool by the counter. The kitchen was mostly unpacked now, but it still looked too cardboard to live in, like if you bumped up against anything too hard, your elbow would go through it.

Rose poured out two mugs of hot milk; then they stirred the cocoa into it, both working determinedly to get the lumps out. Elizabeth looked at the clock—1:05. Outside it was dark, just the orange glow from the streetlights, and lots of dark backyards. Elizabeth's mom brought out the Bailey's, and poured a generous shot into her cocoa.

"Why are we here, mom? I hate this place. Why can't we just go back to Minnesota?" was what Elizabeth wanted to say, but she couldn't. She sipped her cocoa.

Her mom put her hand on Elizabeth's, and said without looking at her, "I just want the best for you, honey." Her mom did that sometimes, answering the questions Elizabeth hadn't asked.

"I know, mom. It'll be fine."

"Sure it will."

At one o'clock in the morning in a cardboard kitchen, neither one of them believed it. They drank for a while.

"Okay, mine first." Rose put her cup down. "I dreamed I was going to work tomorrow, and I was walking into—you never saw *Metropolis*, did you?" Elizabeth shook her head. "We'll have to Netflix it sometime—it's this terrific sci-fi silent from the twenties, German, I think—the robot is very cool. Anyway, there's this scene where all the workers are walking into this huge company, and it's like some huge monster devouring them, and I was in the crowd and I couldn't move, there were so many people around me, I was just carried in the wave towards this door like a mouth, and when I got inside, I looked up above me, and there were teeth. Coming down towards me, enormous teeth. Then I heard you, and I woke up."

"Creepy." Eliz shuddered. "That was a creepy dream."

"And nobody cared. Everybody just walked into it, not caring."

"Gross."

The two of them said it together: "You had a good dream, you had a good dream, you had a good dream, p-tooey." They both turned their heads and pretended to spit. It was supposed to make things better. One of Rose's Jewish friends had shown them that, and they'd done it ever since.

"Okay, now yours." Elizabeth told her about the kid on the bus with the white eyes, and the worms.

"You had a good dream, you had a good dream, you had a good dream, p-tooey," her mom said. "You win, your dream was creepier than mine. Wanna watch TV for a while?"

"Sure." They padded downstairs into what would be the family room when it got unpacked, and curled up on the sofa together sharing a blanket. Elizabeth was surprised to realize she had missed this. She hadn't done this with her mother for a long time.

"What do you want to watch?"

"Nothing scary."

"That's for sure." Rose dug through one of the boxes. "We could watch *Wizard of Oz*. We haven't seen that in a while."

"No, too scary. The witch. And the trees. And the monkeys. And the witch."

"I met the lady who played the witch once in

summer stock. She was playing Madame Arcati in *Blithe Spirit*. She was the sweetest thing—always worried if the apprentices were eating enough. She took me out for a pizza one time—I think to make sure I was eating, but I also think she wanted the company. If you could pick your grandmother, it would have been her."

Elizabeth leaned against her mom. "Remember that time when I was little, and I ran away? You read me *Hansel and Gretel*, and the witch was nearsighted, she had to feel Hansel's finger to see if he was fat enough to eat, and I thought because you wore glasses then, you were a witch. So I ran away. I got almost all the way to Highway 42, and Mrs. Turner saw me walking in the middle of the road crying, and she picked me up. I said 'My mother's a witch,' and she said, 'Oh Betsy, no she isn't, come on, you'll be fine,' and she brought me home. I thought you were a witch, because you were nearsighted."

Rose put her arms around Elizabeth and ruffled her hair. "All of us Callahan women are a little witchy, dear." Then she pulled Elizabeth to her and snuggled her in close. "But that's why I got *Lasik*, my pretty, because you were... RIGHT! Ah-ha-ha-ha-haaaaaaaaa! How about *Princess Bride?*"

## CHAPTER FOUR

# I'm Here

Locked in a keepsake box in a secret desk-drawer is a file of bound emails printed in green ink and tied with a green satin ribbon. The top one reads:

Dear Alberta,

Well, I made it. I'm here. Trip extraordinarily grisly. Gory details to follow.

Here we go again!

L

## CHAPTER FIVE

# Tricky Thing, Light

"Betsy, come on! The bus'll be here any second!" Rose met Elizabeth at the foot of the stairs, a paper bag in her hand.

Elizabeth stopped on the step that put her eye level with her mother, put her backpack down beside her, folded her arms, and took a deep breath. "Mother—" she began. The word "mother" was their signal that they were about to discuss something serious. Rose raised her eyebrows and waited.

Elizabeth went on. "Now that we're in a new place, I feel that this is the time to make a clean start. I don't want to be 'Betsy' anymore. 'Betsy' is a little girl's name. 'Betsys' have 'freckles,' and they get into 'scrapes.' I don't feel like a 'Betsy,' I don't look like a 'Betsy', I haven't felt like a 'Betsy' for years. From now on, I would like to be called, 'Elizabeth.'"

"If you don't mind," she finished.

Rose's eyebrows were all the way up to her hairline,

but underneath them, she had her "trying to be a good mother" face on. "Um, Ok. Sure. Um, it's your name, Bets—er, sorry, um… E-li-za-beth," her mom said the name as if she was pronouncing a word in Swahili. "It's your name. Whatever you, um… sure. Sure." She handed Elizabeth the bag in her hand. "Here's your lunch, first day of school—cold chicken, peanut butter sandwich, two kinds of juice, a banana, bite-size Snickers—"

"Mom, you don't need to, I could do this—"

"I know, E-li-za-beth, I just like to do it for you. Now, give me a hug. I love you, pardner."

"Can I still call you 'pardner'?" Rose pulled Elizabeth's face close and looked her in the eyes. "You're the best thing that ever happened to me, you know? E-li-za-beth?"

"Thanks, mom. I love you too. Good luck on your first day. You look nice."

She did. For the first time in her life, probably, Rose was dressed in a business suit, an electric-blue turquoise that made her eyes flash like neon. She had corralled her hair with a bunch of tortoise-shell combs, and it was working, for the most part.

"Thanks, honey—it's not too grown-up for me?"

"Heck no, mom, you're still a babe."

"Thanks, girlfriend." Another hug. "Now beat it, Bets—um, E-li-za-beth."

Elizabeth went out the door. When she looked back, she saw her mom waving cheerfully with a big toothy smile, the smile she always bit out when she was trying to act brave. Elizabeth smiled the same smile back at her.

Elizabeth felt nervous and out of place, shifting her backpack from one shoulder to the other. A nice, neat suburban neighborhood, nice, neat, perfect lawns; in the driveways, mammoth SUVs and global-warming-conscious hybrids. "Great," she thought. "We're yuppies now."

And here came the nice, neat little school bus, with "Sojourner Truth Magnet School" above the front window. "Hello," said the middle-aged lady driving the bus. "You must be Betsy?"

"Elizabeth, please."

"Welcome aboard, Elizabeth."

And as Elizabeth turns to find a seat, she sees: It's *quiet* in here. The bus is full of kids, but nobody's talking, they're all working—some are on laptops, some on BlackBerries, some are text-messaging each other on their cells.

And there's one kid, a boy, in the back, in a gray sportcoat, black pants, white shirt, earbuds. He's got these zombie dark circles under his eyes, and he's staring at her. Elizabeth freezes: His eyes are white.

No, she lets out her breath again, relieved. He's got pupils like anybody else. It's just a trick of the light. Trick of the light, that's all, just a trick of the light.

Tricky thing, light.

Her heart starts beating again, and she finds an empty seat towards the front and parks. But shivers are running up and down her spine like demented gerbils.

"I think it's important that you have a *look*, and I was naturally attracted to pink because of my outgoing disposition—not a carnation pink, and certainly not Pepto-Bismol, but a bright, bright pink, to complement the color of my eyes, you know what I mean?"

The girl nattering beside Elizabeth was tiny, and had dragged an enormous Nordstrom's bag up the bus steps. A pink tutu was trying to escape from the top. From the bag's weight, it was obvious the tutu was only the top layer.

"See my nails? Bright, bright pink, they're very pretty, thank you, I know, see, they match my sneakers, and my barrettes."

The little girl's name was Penelope. Pink sparkly barrettes held back almost-white curly blonde hair, and watery mint-green eyes were framed by pink cat-eye glasses. "This is my tutu, I have ballet after school today, wanna see my toe shoes?" She started rooting around in the bag, almost disappearing into it. "We're not supposed to have toe shoes yet, but I got some anyway, because all the real ballerinas have them, I walk around in them for exactly fifteen minutes a day, I time it, because I think everyone should have a goal, don't you? I was the Sugar Plum Fairy in the Nutcracker for the BBC."

"The BBC?" Elizabeth's jaw hung open. "I'm impressed."

"You should be. The Barrington Ballet Company is one of the most prestigious ballet schools on the North

Shore. I've done it for two whole years running. Usually the S.P.F.'s in white, but I insisted that she be pink this year, and since my mother was paying for the costumes… see, I even have a pink tiara. And these are *real* rhinestones, not the fake kind."

Elizabeth felt the eyes of the other kids on the bus watching her. First day of school, new kid in town and all, she was glad not to be sitting alone, glad Penelope had sat down next to her, but she felt the other kids watching, and wondered if the little girl in pink was ever going to take a breath—

"I've got Mrs. McCumber for homeroom, who do you have? I'm so glad to have one of the younger teachers, someone who can help me cultivate my personal sense of style—" Elizabeth saw that Penelope did breathe, occasionally, but it didn't seem to slow her down. She seemed harmless enough, like a mosquito, maybe, just buzzing around your ear—

"Here we are, come with me, I'll show you where our homeroom is, and if you have any questions you can just—"

And they stood to get off the bus. As Elizabeth turned to get her things, she looked back at the boy in the back seat. He was just sitting there, looking at her.

He had pupils. Two. Trick of the light. Of course.

## CHAPTER SIX

# Butterfly Tree

The homeroom was cheery, just starting to put up cutouts of pumpkins and ghosts on the bulletin boards—Halloween was a couple of weeks away, they had probably just taken down the September "Welcome back!" stuff.

Mrs. McCumber was pretty, with tight curly black hair and little bright eyes, quick and friendly like a parakeet. Standing beside her at the desk, Elizabeth noticed the handmade "Teacher of the Year" coffee mug, and the shiny red porcelain apple that said "Paris" on its side. "Welcome to our class, Elizabeth. You've missed a bit, not being here at the start of the year, but I'm sure you'll catch up quickly. Did you have a computer lab at your school?"

"Um, yes." Elizabeth didn't tell her that she'd raised the money for the computer lab at R.R.S.L. She looked around. This was a great school. Every desk had a terminal.

Mrs. McCumber smiled. "Well then, I may be asking for your help later, I'm sure you'll be better with computers than I am. Why don't we have you meet the class?"

There were only about twenty students, four rows of five or six, everyone working at their laptops.

"Class, I'd like you to meet Elizabeth Callahan. She's from Minnesota. Elizabeth, why don't you tell us a little bit about yourself?"

Elizabeth had rehearsed her speech. She took out her thumb drive. "I've prepared a short PowerPoint…"

"Elizabeth, we'd really prefer you to just tell us, if you don't mind—"

Elizabeth did mind. Her PowerPoint presentation was spectacular. But she cleared her throat and began.

"My name is Elizabeth, not 'Betsy,' 'Bets,' 'Beth,' 'Bess,' and most-definitely not 'Peg.' I grew up on a farm, I can drive a truck. I am widely known for my organizational skills."

Except for Penelope, none of the kids looked up. Mrs. McCumber said, "I don't think anyone here—I think we're mostly suburbanites. Tell us about life on a farm."

"Well, um…" This was off-topic. Elizabeth ran her thumb against the fingernail of her left ring-finger, to calm herself down. (Elizabeth had nice nails—nine of them. A year ago, they'd been sore-looking, gnawed-on nubs. Chewing her nails helped Elizabeth think, helped her to focus. But on her ninth birthday, Elizabeth had made a deal with herself: She gave herself one fingernail to gnaw on—the ring finger of her left hand. When she needed to gnaw, Mr. Lefty-Ring-Finger was the gnaw-ee. The rest of her nails grew to something that looked like fingernails, at least. Of course, now she had another stress-induced habit: covering up the ring-fingernail of her left hand with her thumb. Elizabeth was okay with that.)

"The farm?" She looked at the cardboard ghost on the bulletin board wearing a derby and saying "Boooooooo!" "—It was nothing special, just about forty acres—the family owned it for eighty years or so. We had horses for a while, but mostly... There were woods, with gullies and a stream, there was the butterfly tree, and mint growing wild, you could smell it at night, and sometimes..."

"Butterfly tree? That sounds interesting. Tell us about that."

Elizabeth cringed. This was not going according to plan. Her nerves had made her blab out something she only shared with her closest friends, not an entire class full of strangers who didn't seem interested enough to look up from their computer screens. But now she was stuck. She dug her fingernail into her thumb.

"There was this tree, where, um... monarchs stopped every year."

"Monarchs?" said Mrs. McCumber, with an encouraging smile.

"Yes, you know, the butterflies. They migrate. From Canada to Mexico every fall. A flock of them. A herd, or whatever. Anyway, they'd stop every year on our tulip tree..."

"A tulip tree?"

"Yes." Elizabeth was perspiring now. "That's the name of it. Because the leaves are shaped like tulips."

"Well, that's very interesting, isn't it, class? Thank you, Elizabeth, we'd love to hear more later on."

That wasn't so bad. Elizabeth looked at the class again. Penelope was beaming at her, nodding her head and making the "thumbs-up" sign. But most of the other students were still staring at their computer screens. Most of them had never even looked up.

But a couple had. One or two of them were looking at her strangely—almost as if they were wondering if she'd be good to eat. What the heck was that?

And both of those kids were dressed in gray.

"Thank you, Elizabeth, you can sit down now. Why don't you take the desk next to Penelope?"

"Mrs. McCumber! Mrs. McCumber!"

One of the gray kids was waving his hand in the air. Elizabeth thought that he looked like that pig in the old cartoons, the one with the stutter—tubby and damp, with hair that looked like it was already starting to get thin. His gray sport coat (who wears a sport coat in fourth grade?) was immaculate, and had a little flag pin on the lapel.

"Yes, Ash, what is it?"

"There's an empty seat next to me, Elizabeth could sit right here," porky-sport-coat-boy beamed.

"Um, it's all right, thanks," said Elizabeth, "I met Penelope on the bus, I'll just sit right here, if that's okay." Elizabeth quickly scooted into the desk next to Penelope.

Penelope whispered, "That was an amazing story, can you really drive a truck?" Elizabeth nodded. She turned around to look back at Ash. He waved chubby fingers at her and winked.

Ewg.

## CHAPTER SEVEN

# Hives

"No thanks, Ambrose, she's not interested," Penelope said to the kid in gray. The boy from the back of the bus was holding out a slip of paper, silently offering it to Elizabeth with a sticky smile. She reached out to accept it, but, "Shoo," Penelope waved him away like a sweat-bee. He tucked the slip of paper back into his pocket, and wandered away without a word.

Elizabeth and Penelope had escaped to the playground when Ash sat down to join them in the lunchroom. They ate together on a bench beside the jungle gyms. It was warm for October, but there was the hint of a chill in the air, so they kept their jackets on. Elizabeth started work on the peanut-butter-and-orange-marmalade sandwich. "What was that about?" she said.

"Who cares?" said Penelope, unpacking her pink-sparkled lunchbox. "When you're as popular as me, you have lots of demands on you. It's a club or something.

They give you this little slip of paper with a URL on it, I must have fifty of them. Would you like a macaroon?"

Elizabeth had never seen pink macaroons before. Penelope nattered on. "You're supposed to go to the website and get the secret handshake or whatever. I told them to stop bothering me." She chewed a slice of apple. "I explained I could never be part of their group. I'm a 'Spring.' Gray washes me out."

"What's the group about?" said Elizabeth.

"Search me. They don't *do* anything. They just get together in their little corner of the playground and tap their BlackBerries and nod their heads. I would hardly find that fulfilling. Your story about the butterflies was trés cool. Why'd you leave Minnesota?"

"My mom got a new job."

"What's she do?"

"She's an advertising executive for Perfect Lady."

"Lyrissa Van Lear? Oooh, she's a personal hero of mine. I greatly admire her sense of style. What does your dad do?"

"No dad."

"No dad?"

"Nope."

"Divorce?"

"Nope."

"Ah."

They chewed for a moment. Elizabeth changed the subject. "Ash is a terrible name."

"Tell me."

"Does everybody call him—"

"They used to. Not so much anymore. He's become, important lately. Somehow. Now he's all active, trying to make 'changes.' Lately he's been trying to convince the school board we should all wear uniforms. 'Better learning environment.' Yuck."

Penelope dusted some pink sprinkles off a cupcake. "Have to watch my girlish figure," she said. "There are *no* chubby ballerinas. You know, you're at a tremendous social disadvantage, not being here at the beginning of the school year, you've missed a great deal. All the best BFFs are already hooked up. Except for me, I'm very selective. I'm going do you a favor and make you my special autumn project."

"Thanks, that'll be nice," said Elizabeth. She wondered if Penelope really had that many people who wanted to be BFFs. "So, if uniforms aren't required, why do so many kids wear gray?"

"Dunno," Penelope munched. "But every day there's a couple more, sitting together, nodding their heads. It's like a science experiment, every day the spot's a little bit bigger. Like mold growing on a slice of bread."

The bell rang, and it was time to go back inside.

Elizabeth needed some fresh school supplies, so she stopped at her locker before she went to class. The hallway smelled of floor wax and gym shoes, and all around her was the sound of slamming lockers and kids coming in from the playground. As she bent down to get the battery-powered pencil sharpener out of her backpack, the light behind her changed. Elizabeth looked up. The kids in gray were in a circle all around her.

Ash was there. He was standing too close, blocking out the light. He leaned in, and Elizabeth could see the sweat on his lip and smell the cafeteria meatloaf on his breath as he smiled and said so quietly she had to strain to hear, "We were told about you, Elizabeth. Told to look out for you. You're *special*. You're a very special young lady, and we really, *really* want you to be part of—"

"—Good afternoon, Mrs. McCumber!" Ash said, turning and smiling to Mrs. McCumber, who had just walked up beside them. "We were just giving Elizabeth a real Sojourner Truth welcome." He reached into a pocket and pressed a slip of paper into Elizabeth's hand. The paper was still warm from Ash's hand, and it was moist.

Ash and the gray kids drifted away like fog. Mrs. McCumber watched them for a moment, then turned to Elizabeth. "Are you all right?" she said.

"What?" said Elizabeth. Why would she not be all right? She looked up at her teacher. Mrs. McCumber looked worried. Why? Why did she look… afraid?

Mrs. McCumber smiled again, and the shadow in her eyes was gone. "What I meant to say, is, how are you liking Sojourner Truth?"

"Everybody seems… very friendly," Elizabeth answered. As she walked back to homeroom with her teacher, she snuck a glance down at the slip of paper in her hand.

There was a URL written on it in green ink.

When Elizabeth got off the bus that day, her mom

was waiting in the truck. She'd changed from her suit into jeans and a tee-shirt—why did her mom look good in everything?—and her hair was pulled back into a ginger ponytail. Elizabeth walked over to the truck's window. A perfunctory kiss. "Get in, pie-face, we're going shopping."

Yow. There was—what? A *tension* in her mom's voice. Had she done something wrong? Elizabeth hurried round the truck, climbed in, and threw her backpack behind the seats, where the gun rack had been when they'd gotten the truck second-hand. Her mom revved the truck as Elizabeth buckled up. As they took the corner, the tires squealed.

Rose hit the play button on the truck's cassette player—The Eagles. This was bad. Something was really bothering her. She turned it up, and yelled over the beginning twangs, "So how was your first day?"

"Great." Now was not the time to tell her mom about the weird, creepy kids in gray. "The school's really nice."

"How's your teacher?"

"Nice. Pretty. Mrs. McCumber."

"Good." Rose was quiet for a while, and Elizabeth looked over at her. Her mom was staring straight ahead and driving, fiercely, her knuckles white against the steering wheel, the muscles in her jaw working.

Elizabeth figured she might as well drop the bomb. "How was your day?" she asked.

"Great!" her mom said, too cheerful and too loud.

Elizabeth tried a joke. "So, was it like your dream?"

"Exactly!" Elizabeth turned, ready to laugh, and stopped herself. Her mom was still staring straight ahead, still clenched. She wasn't kidding.

Elizabeth turned down the music. "Tell me." Her mom was vibrating, she was so—scared? Nervous? Excited? No, she was so *angry* she was ready to bite somebody's head off, but was clamping down on the steering wheel so hard, working so hard not to be furious, it was actually bending a little in her hands.

"It was exactly like the dream. I turn the corner onto the street, and suddenly I'm part of—this sea of workers, all walking towards this big marble façade at the end of the street, over the door it says "Perfection" and everyone around me is balancing their briefcases and their newspapers and trying not to scald themselves with their lattes, and they all seem to be late, and I'm the only one wearing a color, I'm being carried along in this sea of gray like a pine cone in a river, I look up and we're all being funneled into this big mouth, just kidding, it's just a door, a series of doors, we're all flowing towards this series of doors at the top of a flight of green marble stairs, but I tell you, BetsyElizabeth, when I got to those doors, just like in the dream, I looked up and *I expected to see teeth*."

"So, I have my own office, with my name on the door, you have to come down and see it, but not for a little while, let me get a little more settled, and after lunch one of the Kyles—all these guys dressed in gray sharkskin named Kyle, how can so many guys can be named Kyle?—sat me down and told me without telling me that it might be a good idea to try to 'fit in' with the Perfection color-scheme, or rather the *non-color scheme*—gray, gray, gray, the only one allowed to wear colors is Miss Van Lear, 'She Who Must be Obeyed,' I don't know what that refers to, but it's what they all call her behind her back."

"Did you meet her?"

"Yes, she came by and said an official hello, it was a little weird meeting her—she's... you know how some people are bigger than others? Well, she's... *large*. It's like meeting the Grand Canyon, or something. Hoover Dam. She takes up a lot of space. But she was very nice, told me how glad she was to have me aboard, here where she could 'keep an eye on me' is actually what she said, and how she was looking forward to getting to know me better, I'm invited to join her for tea tomorrow after work, you ever notice how sometimes you feel like there's *more going on* than you know about? Like there's a whole 'nother *reality* that nobody's bothered to tell you? That's how I feel there. And she never goes anywhere without this bunch of yappy little white dogs."

"After lunch, *another* one of the Kyles came by and stressed the importance of being a *team player*, and of *fitting in*, how important it was to be part of the Perfection *team*, and how we all have to work *together—*"

"Like one big happy family?"

"No, honey, like a *hive*."

When she turned back to the road, she forgot to stop smiling. For a while, Rose drove along in silence, grinning like the Joker. "Let's go to the mall and get me some gray clothes!"

Elizabeth figured her mom had her own problems. She decided not to tell her about her own weird day at school.

Elizabeth didn't know that things were about to get a whole lot weirder.

## CHAPTER EIGHT

# Salutations, Small Mortal

That evening, Elizabeth decided to try the URL and see what all the fuss was about. The computer was on the floor, and Elizabeth sat cross-legged on her sleeping bag in front of it. She pulled the slip of paper out of her pocket. The address was written in green ink: uraspecialkid.com.

Catchy, bouncy music, and an animated cat boarded onto the screen, dressed in skater gear, his pants bagging around his knees. "Greetings, small human!" he grinned out at her, in a friendly older-brother sort of way. "Before we get started, click and let me know: be you a wee dude or dude-erina?"

Elizabeth hated this kind of pretend-hip patronizing. But she wondered what would happen, so she clicked "wee dude," just to see.

The screen exploded with a blast of bombs and gunfire, and she was hurtling along in a dangerously swerving war vehicle of some sort, blowing things up, dinosaurs and zombies, for the most part.

"Um-hmm," she said to herself. "Boy-stuff. Thought so." She closed the website down.

Then she re-entered it, clicking "dude-erina" this time.

There was beautiful music, and the screen filled with rainbows and dancing unicorns and big-eyed kitties. She didn't usually like this kind of thing, but this time, Elizabeth felt… relaxed. Comfortable. Cared for. Like she was settling into a warm, soothing bubble bath, and everything was fine, really kind of dreamy, and all the questions and problems of the day were melting away, and she felt the tension flowing out of her as the music smoothed out everything, and she was being cradled in the warmest, coziest blanket of the most wonderful, the smoothest, the softest—

Then, suddenly the screen blacked out, and Elizabeth was under icy, dark water, choking, the surface impossibly far above her, she was struggling to get to air, her throat filled with brackish, foul-tasting water, coughing and gagging, as she kicked, struggled, spasmed to the surface where air might be and she gulped—

Harsh, bright light. Her eyes opened. Elizabeth was back in her bedroom.

"Sorry, BetsyElizabeth, I was using the hair dryer and making popcorn at the same time. Must have blown a circuit breaker. Hope you didn't lose anything important. Are you okay?"

What had happened? Her mom was standing in the door of Elizabeth's bedroom, drying her hair. The screen before Elizabeth was dark now, shut off by the power outage.

Elizabeth's head was spinning. She tried to tell her mom about the website, but something inside her wouldn't let her. She opened her mouth to try again, but the words wouldn't come; it was like she couldn't, somehow. "Don't want to worry anybody, don't want to worry anybody, don't want to worry anybody," the thought flashed again and again in screaming neon across her mind. Elizabeth breathed deep and tried to look like nothing had happened. "Yeah, mom, I'm… fine. Yeah. Fine."

"Well, don't stay up too late. Sleep tight, pardner. Sweet dreams."

"You too, mom."

What had just happened? Elizabeth wasn't sure, but she felt like she'd had… a close call. She turned out the light and lied awake for a while, wondering, looking at the patterns of light the streetlamps cast on the plaster sworls of the ceiling.

"Kid! Hey, Kid!" thumpthumpthump.

Oh great, *this* dream again. Elizabeth opened one eye—she'd forgotten to turn her monitor off, and the room was dimly lit by its glow. She rolled over to look at the screen and nearly jumped out of her sleeping bag.

Her monitor screen was filled with a face.

A big face that looked at her and said, "Betsy!"

"Elizabeth," she replied, automatically.

"Let us through!"

"Excuse me?"

"Let us through!" The voice was muffled, like it was inside a box, or on the other side of a glass window…

"I don't know what you're talking about, but just on general principles, no way," said Elizabeth.

Another face crowded in beside the first one. Two pillows, it looked like, with eyes and mouths flattened against the glass of her computer screen. The one who was talking had a button sewed on for a nose.

"Betsy, you've got to let us through! There isn't much time!"

"Uh-huh. And you would be who, exactly?"

"Don't ask, don't ask, there isn't time! You've got to invite us through! Right now!" Then the button-face started rhyming:

*"It's urgent! It's pressing! It's serious, grave,*
*Compelling, essential, there's no time to shave!"*

Elizabeth nodded. "Uh-huh. This is really interesting. I'm sure that when I wake up, I'm going to—"

"It's not a dream! We're—"

"Move over, sweetie, let me." The painted-looking face crowded out the button-nose. "Little girl, lookit, you're giving us—my lovely companion here is right, there is not much time. Ask us through, already."

"Why?"

"Because the fate of your cockamamie world is at stake!"

Ok. Too weird now. Back to bed. Elizabeth reached out to turn off the computer.

# "NOOOOO!!!!!!"

"All right." Elizabeth pulled back her hand. She felt calm. Since this was a dream, what did she have to lose? "What did you want me to do, again?"

The button-nose nudged back onto the screen again. "You have to ask us through, Betsy, invite us in."

Elizabeth thought, since this was a dream, why the heck not?

"And how do I do that?"

The two faces said in unison:

## "YOU HIT ENTER!"

Elizabeth did.

There was a flash of light and a poof of cinnamony-smelling smoke and Elizabeth was laying on her back on the floor, looking up at two—whats?

They were both about the size of sixth-graders—five-foot-six or so, a few inches taller than Elizabeth. One was noisily colored, wearing a dress that looked like it had been made from an old patchwork quilt. The other was drabber, with old, patched, faded-blue clothes and a floppy hat. He wore gloves, and there was straw sticking out of them.

Their faces were—friendly, but unusual, to say the least. The one with the straw had a face that looked like it had been not-very-carefully painted on an old burlap sack. One side of his—his? Elizabeth guessed, he *was* wearing pants—one side of his mouth was painted higher than the other, and one eye was bigger. It made him look a little drunk. The other—a female, it must be, she *was* wearing a dress—she had buttons for eyes and nose (they didn't match) sewn onto a head that looked like it might have been a pillow once, with a generous ponytail of bright orange yarn sewed onto the top. They both looked like big, homemade, badly-stuffed toys.

They smiled down at her, friendly, but a little worried-looking.

"Stand back. Give the kid some air," said the crow perched on the straw man's shoulder.

The talking crow did it. If this dream was going to be this interesting, she didn't want to miss any of it. Elizabeth sat up.

"Finally." The straw man held out a straw-stuffed hand, made from an old cotton work-glove. He swept off his hat and bowed from the waist, shaking Elizabeth's hand formally. "Salutations, small mortal," he said.

"Um, hi," said Elizabeth.

"I'm the Scarecrow, and this is Scraps. We're from Oz."

# CHAPTER NINE

# Recycling

Another green-inked email, bound in a green ribbon:

Dear Alberta,

Well, getting here was not half the fun. It was no fun at all.

Again, and again, and again... you remember how unpleasant it can be—that moment of quiet and darkness after all the fuss, and that slightly bored, kindergarten-teacher voice: "Umm-hmm, and what did we learn *this* time?"

And then screaming "NOTAGAINNNNN!!!!" And they always tell you, move towards the light, and of course we don't, we go the other way, spiraling into the dark and getting whirled

around like being flushed through the inside
of a tuba.

And then the baby-poo-green Waiting Room with
the vinyl furniture and the ashtray no one
empties. Then Counseling. Lots of sympathetic
head-shaking, tsk-tsk, there, there, calm
down, have a cup of tea. They did what? Dear,
dear. Here's a Kleenex. Blow.

And then the big question: Well, what do you
think you want to do now?

And the wolverine in the gut so angry we can
barely see, it erupts out of us like a star
going nova, scorching everything nearby to
cinders:

I want **REVENGE**.

Are you sure, dear? Again? Does that seem like
a good choice to you? Wouldn't you like to
think about it for a bit? Perhaps let bygones
be bygones this time and just move on? No?
Well, if that's what you want, I'm sure you
know best, shuffling through the tin box full
of penciled index cards, well, this place is
very popular—

# The Hackers of Oz

And then getting flushed through the tuba again, and here we are once more, blinking, nauseated, opening our eyes in a new place with a new body, and the worst hangover of several lifetimes.

Ready to start again.

There has got to be an easier way.

Xox,
L


PS—Yes, I know, but when you really stop to think about it, people come and go pretty quickly everywhere, don't they?

## CHAPTER TEN

# Bad Poetry and Red Velvet

Elizabeth awoke the next morning. As she looked up through her still-curtainless window, the sky was a cheery, bright, scrubbed-clean Crayola blue. Elizabeth just lay in her sleeping bag for a moment, enjoying the warmth and remembering her whacko dream from the night before. She smiled, and shook her head. Mom was never going to believe this one.

"I think she's awake."

"How can you tell?"

"She stopped snoring."

Elizabeth rolled over. The Scarecrow and the patchwork girl were inches away, studying her earnestly. The crow was pooping on her dresser. Elizabeth jumped up and yelped.

"Who are you? Get the heck out of my room!"

"Sweetie, that's illogical," said the Scarecrow. "If we get the heck out of your room, we will not be able to tell you who we are. Of course, a discussion through a crack in the door might be a possibility, but really—"

*"Betsy, Betsy, all upset-sy!*

*Careful, or you'll Betsy-wetsy!*

Don't get your panties in an uproar, Bets," the patch-work girl said. "There's nothing to get excited about."

"But you—who—? Mo-oooom—"

"Shh-shh-shh!" The two figures piled on top of her, pressing stuffed fingers over her mouth. "We met last night. I'm the Scarecrow, this is Scraps? We're from Oz?"

Elizabeth fell back onto her sleeping bag with a thud. She felt sorry for herself, all of a sudden: poor Elizabeth, she showed such promise, such an organized little girl, but then she went crazy when she got into the fourth grade.

The patchwork girl dropped to the floor next to her. She was soft, it didn't make much noise. The Scarecrow knelt beside her.

"We thought you'd be taller," said Scraps.

The crow on her dresser cleared his throat noisily. "Don't bother to introduce the bird. Really, it's fine. The bird is used to it. Just ignore the bird."

"Sorry. This is Oscar." The Scarecrow rolled his eyes and whispered, "Crows can be so sensitive."

"Raven. Get it right, straw-for-brains. I'm a raven."

"Big crow, same deal."

"Not the same. Same genus, completely different species." The raven neatened up a chest feather with his beak. "Pleased to meet you, missy."

Elizabeth looked from one to the other. If she was going to go crazy, she could do worse. This delusion was entertaining, at least. They seemed friendly, like puppies, eager. The Scarecrow seemed to be the one in charge, or at least, the one who thought he was. Despite his— goofy, really—painted-on smile, he was staring at her seriously. Some straw dropped onto her sleeping bag.

"Little girl, you have a tremendous responsibility."

Oh, terrific, Elizabeth thought. Not only was she going crazy, now she had responsibilities. "What?"

"Relax, it's nothing serious." The patchwork girl— Scraps, of course her name was Scraps, why wouldn't it be?—leaned in close. There was something about her— maybe her smile. Or maybe the crazy riot of color from the—quilt that she was made of. But something about her made Elizabeth feel better, made her feel like—like what? Comfortable. Like someone you meet for the first time, but you feel you've been friends forever.

"Nothing serious? That's a relief."

"You've only gotta save the world." Scraps nodded at her, cheerily.

"Look, you guys'll just have to go back wherever you came from. I have school."

"Darling, that's impossible, unless you've got a tornado in your pocket," said the Scarecrow. "There's no way back. At least not for now. And getting here was complicated enough."

"Can't you just climb back into—" Elizabeth waved vaguely at the computer screen.

"Nope! We're here, we're queer! Get used to it!" The patchwork girl stood and spun around with her arms spread out.

"I don't think that means what you think it does," said the crow.

The patchwork girl thumbed her nose at him, and said:

*"Who cares, ya big drip,*
*We're on a road trip!"*

Then all three of them yelled together really loud, "ROAD TR-I-I-I-P!"

Wha—? There was a knock on the bedroom door. "BetsyElizabeth—turn off the computer and get a move on, girl. You're going to miss the bus."

The door opened. "Oh, you're up already." Rose, dressed in her new gray work outfit, was trying to push her hair into something businesslike. She looked into the room. "Ah. See you've finally started to unpack. Hmm—I don't remember those..."

Elizabeth looked—Scraps and the Scarecrow had flung themselves into a corner, piled on top of each other with arms and legs all over the place, and looked like two large stuffed toys. The raven was nowhere to be seen. When Rose turned her back, Scraps stuck out her tongue at Elizabeth. It was made of red velvet.

"Well, don't dawdle, you don't want to be late. Where did I leave those earrings?" Rose walked down the hall, and Elizabeth closed the door. The raven walked out of the closet. "Where did you learn to do that?"

"We saw it in a movie once," said Scraps. The Scarecrow and raven joined her: "Phone home!"

"You have mov—?" Elizabeth stopped herself, and got very serious. "I'm not imagining this, am I?"

Scraps, the Scarecrow, and the raven shook their heads.

"You're really here?"

Scraps, the Scarecrow, and the raven nodded.

"All right, then listen." Elizabeth stretched up to her full four-foot-ten, and pointed a stern finger at them. "I know I'm going to regret this, but the two of—the three of you have to stay in here and wait for me to come home. And then you've got some 'splaining to do. Got it?"

Scraps, the Scarecrow, and the raven nodded again.

"Promise?"

They crossed their hearts, or where their hearts would have been if—

Enough, too much to deal with. For a few minutes, Elizabeth tried to get ready, pretending very hard that they weren't there. Then she gave up and took her clothes into the bathroom to change. He was a boy scarecrow after all. Did scarecrows have gender? The raven sounded like a—oh, too complicated. She was only ten. Her head hurt.

When she went to school, she closed the door firmly behind her. As she closed it, all three of them smiled and waved—two gloved hands waving hopefully in the air, and one large, glossy, black-feathered wing.

## CHAPTER ELEVEN

# The URL

In a way, Elizabeth was having a very satisfying day. She was a world-class worrier; it was nice to have a project that really tested the limits of her skills. She spent the whole morning stewing about her insanity—Would she have to wear a straitjacket? Would they have one in her size? Would she look good in it? Would the food in the asylum be alright? Would she have to eat gruel?—so the time or two she'd been called on in class, her answers didn't make much sense, and Mrs. McCumber looked at her strangely. Penelope whispered answers, but Elizabeth was too busy, and Mr. Ringfinger got a thorough workout through four class periods.

At lunch she just wanted to be alone to be able to really concentrate on her worrying. So, she ditched Penelope and sat on a bench by herself, gumming her peanut-butter sandwich, contemplating the Looney Bin. How was she going to gently break it to her mother that she was nuts?

The day was—spooky, which helped her mood. It was foggy, a weird low-lying fog so thick that Elizabeth would sometimes just see a pair of legs running along, or a hat floating by, or a basketball dribbling itself, and people appeared and disappeared in the cloudy gray like ghosts. And it was quiet—the fog soaked up the sound, so it was almost like she was watching a silent movie, or something on TV with the sound turned off. Elizabeth saw Penelope off by the jungle gyms by herself in her pink tutu, listening to her iPod. Every now and then, she'd rise up on her toes. She must have been practicing for ballet class. Watching her was like flipping through the pictures in an album: Penelope would strike a pose, then vanish for a moment as the fog stole her away, and when the fog rolled back, she'd be in another pose, in another place.

There were a lot of gray kids around today, clumping together in twos or threes. They would gather and put their heads together like ants rubbing their antennae, then the fog would close over them and they'd be gone.

Elizabeth watched—it was hypnotic, the silent dance the fog revealed and concealed. She saw the gray kids clumping together in larger and larger groups, and they seemed to be moving in one direction, as if some silent agreement had been made. Elizabeth realized with horror that they were moving closer and closer, closing together on *Penelope* as she practiced. There was a circle of gray kids around her, drawing closer, closing in, tightening around her like a claw.

Then Elizabeth couldn't see Penelope's pink toe

shoes anymore, they were lost in a clot of gray and black slacks surrounding her, gray and black getting tighter and tighter. Elizabeth stood up to cry something, to warn Penelope, of what? She didn't know. It was like a nightmare where she tried to cry out, tried to wake herself up, screamed, but no sound came out. There wasn't any sound, just a damp, foggy quiet, weird echoes coming from nowhere, but Elizabeth thought she heard a fragment of something that sounded like, "No, you can't make me! I'm a *Spring*!" and something else that sounded like "*white eyes like bats*—" but the fog had rolled over the scene, burying it in a cold, suffocating blanket of mist.

When it rolled back again, the kids in gray were gone, and there was a pink smudge on the cement.

Elizabeth ran over. Penelope was twitching and rolling back and forth on the ground, talking to herself. Bubbles of spit burbled at the corner of her mouth.

"Penelope! Are you okay?" Elizabeth knelt over her, terrified, slapping one of her cheeks gently. Penelope didn't hear her, didn't meet her eyes, just rocked, her face frozen in an unblinking, wide-eyed smile. There was a puddle of drool beside her on the concrete.

"Mrs. McCumber! Anybody! Help!" Elizabeth ran.

It didn't take long for the ambulance to get there. Teachers clustered around Penelope, tucking a blanket around her; Principal Burmeister knelt beside her, patting her hand. Elizabeth overheard one of them saying she must have fallen, must have hit her head or something.

The ambulance crept silently onto the playground, Mars Lights flashing weirdly in the fog. The paramedics shined lights into Penelope's eyes, then bundled her up on a stretcher and loaded her gently into the ambulance. Elizabeth found the pink cat-eye glasses, and handed them to the driver. One of the lenses was shattered, and there was a spider-web pattern on the glass.

As they lifted Penelope onto the stretcher, she turned her head, and a wet, balled-up piece of paper rolled out of her mouth onto the ground. Elizabeth saw it, and picked it up. As the ambulance sped away, she unrolled it.

It was the URL.

## CHAPTER TWELVE

# It Is Possible That Mistakes Might Have Been Made

"All right, spill it."

Elizabeth sat cross-legged on the floor in her room, with a chair wedged under the doorknob and her back against the wall. The two stuffed figures sat across from her on her sleeping bag. The raven was pecking at the button-eyes on one of Elizabeth's old dolls.

After Penelope was driven away, school let out early, so after the bus dropped her off, Elizabeth had some time before Rose got home. She'd opened the door of her bedroom hoping that the shock of what had happened to Penelope would have cleared her mind. She hoped that her bedroom would be empty: there would be no animated bed-spreads or straw men or talking birds.

# It Is Possible That Mistakes...

But they were all right where she'd left them, sitting on her sleeping bag with their hands clasped in their laps, waiting for her like obedient kindergartners. Elizabeth's heart sank. But, she'd had time to think about it riding home on the bus. She adjusted her glasses on her nose, and took out her index cards with her list of questions.

"All right. Who are you?"

The two stuffed figures whispered anxiously. Scraps turned to her. "Bets, we're a little concerned. We told

you twice." She spelled in out slowly, pointing: "He's... the Scarecrow... I'm... Scraps... we're... from Oz."

"Don't mention the bird. No need. The bird's not important," the raven sulked.

Elizabeth ignored him. "Oz? You mean like, *The Wizard of Oz? That* Oz?"

The Scarecrow turned to Scraps. "Finally, she got it."

"But that's... that's a movie."

"Darling, just because it's a movie, doesn't mean it's not true."

"You're *that* Scarecrow?"

"Yup."

"Wanna sing a little something?"

"Just because it's in the movie doesn't mean it *is* true, either. Liberties were taken."

"Okay. And why are you here?"

Scraps and the Scarecrow conferred again. "To help you save your world."

"From what?"

"We don't know! Really!" the Scarecrow said. He was getting upset, and starting to shed, sweating wisps of straw that floated in the air around him. "We were hoping you would know. We only know that there isn't much time. It's *terribly urgent*. There's a great disturbance in The Force."

Elizabeth bit her lip. "Isn't that from another movie?"

"Well, who doesn't like *Star Wars*? Well, at least the first three—"

"And it's my responsibility to save the world?"

"Yup. Sorry."

"Why me?"

The Scarecrow suddenly became very interested in picking up the bits of straw and stuffing them back into his sleeves. "Um, we're a little unclear on that, as well."

Elizabeth folded her arms. "Tell me what you know."

The Scarecrow wrung his gloved hands, twisting soft fingers together. "Well, here's what we think," he mumbled to the floor, not meeting Elizabeth's eyes. "It is possible that Mistakes Might Have Been Made."

Elizabeth waited.

"You know how in the movie, munchkin, munchkin, munchkin, big soap bubble, singing, dancing, yellow brick road, etc? Houses falling on people? PO'd green ladies in black?"

Elizabeth waited.

"Well, a good deal of that was MGM. The singing and dancing, especially."

He continued. "But there was truth in it, too. And, um, there *might, perhaps, maybe, could have been, one or two* <u>mistakes</u> *that might have been* made. Perhaps it would be easier if we—"

"Blah blah blah," said the raven. "Are we gonna watch the movie or aren't we?"

CHAPTER THIRTEEN

# Da Duh Da-Dit, Da Daaaa-Da

"We may not have time to see the whole thing. My mom'll be home pretty soon."

They sat on the couch in what would eventually be the family room. Elizabeth sat between Scraps and the Scarecrow. She had a brand-new legal pad on her lap, and beside her, a handful of dangerously-sharpened pencils.

The Scarecrow held the remote. "Now remember, Elizabeth, it's a movie. It's a dramatization. There were liberties taken, for dramatic effect. It's called 'artistic license.'"

"Do I have an Artistic License?" asked Scraps.

"Shh," Elizabeth answered. She turned to the Scarecrow. "So you've seen this movie before?"

"Of course, it's one of our favorites. This and *Octopussy*. Scraps is very fond of the young Sean Connery."

Scraps pretzeled her arms together. "He's dreamy!"

"How do you get movies in Oz?"

"Netflix, same as you. We're not that far away. That's part of the problem."

On the not-very-large TV screen, a lion roared. Elizabeth settled back. She hadn't seen the movie in a couple of years.

The Scarecrow hit the remote. "Fast forward, fast forward, fast forward—okay, I gotta ask—does Kansas really look like this? All gray and everything?"

"Of course not. It's colored just like the rest of the world. Flat. But colored."

"Thanks, I always wondered about that."

"So they're using an Artistic License," said Scraps. "How can I get an Artistic License?"

"Shh," explained Elizabeth.

"Pudgy little girl, barky dog, running down the road, old lady tending chickens, song song song—" The Scarecrow stopped talking, and they all listened until bluebirds flew.

"Awww," the Oz folk sighed. "Nice song."

"That girl had some pipes," said the raven.

"Yup," said the Scarecrow. He turned to Elizabeth. "Your grandmother couldn't sing nearly that well." He turned back to the TV. "Scary lady on a bicycle." Scraps and the Scarecrow did the song, "Da duh da-dit, da DAAAA-da—"

"Wait a minute." Elizabeth took the remote from his hand and froze the playback. "What did you say?"

"Da duh da-dit, da DAAAA-da—"

"No, before that. Something about my *grandmother*?"

"Sorry," said the Scarecrow. "I guess it would be your *great*-grandmother."

"What do you mean?"

"Your great-grandmother was Dorothy," said Scraps. "Shh. We're getting to the good part." She took the remote and started it up again.

Elizabeth didn't really see much of the next few minutes. She didn't see Miss Gulch taking the dog, or the dog's heroic escape, or the little girl's—*her great-grandmother's*—decision to run away. Elizabeth sat there with her mouth open, trying to put things together in her head.

This movie had always been a family favorite, but her mom had never mentioned—Elizabeth wondered if she knew? That this movie wasn't just a really good old movie, it was *history*? *Her family's* history? Her middle name *was* Gale, so that's where it came from. She'd always thought it was her great-grandmother's *first* name, she didn't know it was her *last* name...

Suddenly this was important. Elizabeth sat up straighter and started to take notes.

The Scarecrow saw what she was doing. "Oh, you don't need to write this stuff down. This is just MGM. It isn't really true."

"Not true?"

"Nope, Miss Gulch, Professor Marvel, running away—they're just setting up the story. Artistic—"

"Artistic License," said Scraps. "Shh, we know."

"So this stuff wasn't in the book?"

"Nope. And there's lots in the book that didn't make it into the movie.

The book is a *little* more accurate, although L. Frank Baum also took—oh, here's the tornado. Now that part is true."

"This isn't possible."

"Oh, yes, it can be. Tornadoes are weird. Lots of people have survived tornado-rides."

"Well, if Oz is someplace you can get by tornado, it's not that far away."

"Didn't I just say that? Okay, here we are in Oz."

"Does it really look like this?"

"Parts of it. But they have the Munchkin country all wrong, of course—it's mostly blue. One of those Technicolor things, most likely—it was a new process, they were probably trying to show off. Ok, here comes Glinda. Bossy lady. Nice, but bossy."

"She doesn't really travel by bubble, does she?"

"Not usually. Occasionally—parties and things. Weddings."

"Does she really look like that?"

"Oh, yes. She's a very snappy dresser. The hat's a little bigger. Now this actress, Billie Burke, was a famous New York stage actress, married to Flo Ziegfeld. She was later in the *Topper* movies. All right, so now, the witch comes in."

Scraps catapulted over the back of the couch and hid behind it. "Tell me when she's gone!"

Elizabeth watched the cyanide-green witch, a terrifying swirl of black scarves and nastiness. "Was she really that bad?"

"Oh, yes, this part is practically a documentary. All right, the shoes. The shoes, the shoes, the shoes. What a mess, all over a pair of shoes. If she'd just given her the shoes then, I mean they *were* her sister's shoes, this whole thing—oh, well. No use crying over spilt footwear." The Scarecrow chuckled to himself, and was disappointed when no one else joined him. "Also, they weren't really 'ruby.'"

The witch disappeared in a ball of flame. "Okay, Scraps, you can come out now." Scraps peeked over the edge of the couch, making sure the witch was gone. When she sat down again, she took Elizabeth's hand. The Scarecrow continued. "The lady who played the witch was badly burned when they shot that. She went to the hospital and couldn't return to shooting for weeks."

"You sure know a lot of Oz trivia."

"*Trivia*? Excuse me? *Trivia*? Young lady, these are *important facts*. In Oz, they teach them *in school*. In Oz, the names of your *presidents* is trivia."

"Sorry. So, everyone knows the movie pretty well?"

"Oh, yes, we watch it every year when it comes on."

"You get TV?"

"Sure. Most of it's amazingly stupid. But this we watch every year. Also, we're very fond of South Park. And American Idol, of course."

"Ryan Seacrest is dreamy!" said Scraps, pretzeling her arms again.

"All right, dancing dancing dancing, yellow brick road, dancing dancing—Now here is where I first met your great—"

"I love this part!" Scraps bounced up and down on the couch.

"Me, too," said Oscar.

The Scarecrow cleared his throat. "Yes, well—"

Scraps cooed,

*"Coo-coo-ca-choo! He just won't do!*
*Ray Bolger's not as dreamy as you!"*

"Yeah, you're a dreamboat," said the raven.

The Scarecrow's burlap face pinked a little. How was that possible, Elizabeth wondered.

"Yes, well, this part is pretty much as it was, Tin Woodsman, oil can, witch, ball of fire never happened, lion, funny song in a Bronx dialect, hilarious. Never happened, never happened, never happened—poppies... getting out of there was *much* more complicated than that... Emerald City. Okay, now here, MGM kind of misses the point. See, at that time, the reason that it was called 'the Emerald City' was because we all had to wear these green glasses, see, at that time the Wizard wasn't even a Wiz *at all* to speak of, so, we all got these green glasses when we came in, and that turned the whole city green."

"So that was all a fake?"

"It was then. That's how it looks now. Gentrification."

The Oz folk all watched in silence for a moment, as the four travelers skipped towards the gorgeous green city glowing on the horizon. They sighed. Elizabeth was surprised—she could actually feel how homesick they were, sitting beside them on the couch.

"Witch on the broomstick skywriting, never happened, big talking head, artistic license, we all saw him separately, fast forward here, okay... the witch."

"I'll be back here if you need me," said Scraps from behind the couch.

"Scary. Very scary. And not just the monkeys— wolves and bees, too. But the monkeys were the worst. They smelled incredibly bad, I'm told." He pointed at his painted-on nose. "Don't breathe, can't smell. MGM cleaned them up a lot for the movie, gave them those cute little outfits." The Scarecrow watched in silence for a moment, as Ray Bolger was dismembered by the flying monkeys. "I hate this part."

"This has to be artistic license," said Elizabeth.

"Oh no, that's pretty much the way was. It was extremely embarrassing. I ended up in a tree. At least part of me. Fast forward, fast forward, never happened, never happened... Okay." He paused the playback and turned to Elizabeth.

"*This* is where we *might have* gone wrong. *This* is where mistakes perhaps *might have* been made. Yes, a bucket of water was thrown, and, yes, a witch was melted, <u>but</u>: we *may have* made a slight miscalculation."

"The witch wasn't really melted?"

"Oh, she was melted. Terrible mess. Completely ruined the rug. And then we all went dancing back to the Emerald city, thinking all of our problems were over. We thought, throw some water on her, dissolve the witch, problem solved, happy ending, right? Wrong."

He continued. "See, what we've learned since then, is—you know how Einstein says—okay, it's like this: When you dissolve, or fricassee, or chop into little bits, whatever, a witch, the energy—"

Elizabeth knew this from science class: "The energy isn't destroyed, it's just transformed?"

"Kind of. But it's worse than that."

"How?"

"Einstein sugarcoated it. With witches, you destroy a witch, the energy isn't just transformed."

"What is it?"

"It's *distilled*."

"Oh. You mean—"

"Yeah, they just come back again, meaner and meaner each time."

"Oh. That could be a problem."

"Yes. Each time they come back, they're <u>worse</u>."

They were all quiet for a while. Elizabeth put down her pencil and her legal pad and looked at the Scarecrow. "So, um… what are you doing *here*?"

The Scarecrow looked back at her solemnly. "Elizabeth, I think you already know what we *suspect*, what we *fear* might be happening. But we don't *know*. That's what we're here to find out." He took Elizabeth's hands in his. "Do you have any *easy* questions?"

Elizabeth had a thousand, but none of them were easy. She said, "It's not important, but—you said the slippers weren't 'ruby.' What color were they?

"Silver," said the Scarecrow.

Then his brow furrowed. "But Elizabeth, darling, it's nearly seven o'clock. Shouldn't your mother have been home by now?"

## CHAPTER FOURTEEN

# GLGs

Dear Alberta,

Wish you were here. You really must come and visit, when you get a little time off—it looks like I've finally found a world that's going to work this time...

You know what a nightmare it's been, over and over—just when things finally start going your way, another GLG comes skipping down some damn road or other, and the next thing you know, a fat-legged child-star is daintily toe-stepping her pudgy little hooves around a smoking puddle of *you*, and they're mopping you off the floor with a squeegee. Fudge.

GLGs. "Who would've thought that a Good Little Girl like you could destroy all my beautiful, etc., etc." GLGs, golden curls bouncing in slow motion as they gambol in the sunshine, flashing their vicious little baby teeth. We all suffer the curse of the GLGs, but you have to admit I've had it worse than most:

I'm coming into the castle room, a song in my heart, a cackle on my lips and a blood-filled hourglass in my hand, and as I open the door, I hear the scrape of metal above me. I do a slow-motion look up: the oldest trick in the book, a bucket on the door over my head, tipping towards me in slow motion, turning over and over—

Fudge.

Or, as I'm coming into the room, some genius has put a well-placed bar of soap in front of the door, and I go skating across the castle floor like a clown on a banana peel, crashing into the waiting bucket, which somersaults into the air, slowly turning over and over—

Fudge.

Or the time they were waiting for me with the lawn sprinkler.

And let's not even talk about the super-
soakers.

But this time it's going to be different. This
time I've outsmarted them with some protective
camouflage. This time I've become the Goodest
Little Girl of all.

And best of all, in this world, they've
invented something wonderful called... *"water-
proofing."*

Wickedly,
L

## CHAPTER FIFTEEN

# Mine

Rose stood outside the brownstone on Castlewood Street. It was a quiet street, big old trees and moneyed mansions, and rich enough to be a cul-de-sac; the people here must like their street quiet, without any vulgar traffic, she thought. It was a dark night—no moon yet, and the streetlights here were charming old antiques, probably more for show than for light. Rose looked at the imposing steps leading up to the imposing porch—some architect had put two very alive-looking gargoyles above it. They glared down at her. Rose swallowed, walked up the steps, and pressed the bell.

Sonorous. Deep within the brownstone, an impossibly large gong sounded like the heartbeat of a brontosaurus. Rose waited for a moment, and ran her hand over her hair, checking it once again. It was still perfect, mostly. She was still wearing her new business suit— gray, like all of them at *Perfection*, but of a nubby, rich-looking raw silk. She was excited—this meeting could possibly be very *important*.

The door opened, and things got weird.

Behind the door was an odd-looking little... *person* in a faded cotton house-dress. The... *person* was very small, barely the size of Betsy when she was eight. The person's eyebrows met in a single thick, hairy line; the eyes beneath them were crafty, tiny and deep-set; and the mouth was—wide. Very. The person had large ears, and—her?—head came to a definite—point, accented by a tuft of hair and a little pink satin bow smudged with dirty fingerprints.

Rose tried not to stare. "Um, I'm here to see Miss Van Lear? I'm expected."

The person didn't speak, but smiled a *wiiiiide* smile that was not at all welcoming, the teeth behind it were too big, and gestured for Rose to come in. The person then got close, very close, and looked up into Rose's face. Rose couldn't be sure, but she thought she was being *smelled*. The person gestured for Rose to follow. She did, and the huge, thick door closed behind her like the door of a tomb.

Rose followed as the person scuttled down a narrow hallway lined with textured wallpaper the color of clotted blood. It was lit, dimly, by antique sconces, wonders of tortured glass and metal, and you couldn't see the ceiling, it was too high. At the end of the hall was an old elevator, the kind in European hotels in the movies. The gate was iron, painted green, and once Rose was inside it, the door closed with a clanging snap. It felt like a cage.

The person pushed a lever, and the elevator shuddered to life.

"Have you worked for Miss Van Lear long?" The person laughed at this; the hissing, voiceless laugh was even less pleasant than the smile, so Rose rode the rest of the way in silence. The ride took a lot longer than Rose expected—from the outside, the house had seemed a normal height for the neighborhood, three stories at most. But the little green cage went up and up, forever.

Finally, it jolted to a stop, and the person opened the door. Rose stepped out a little faster than was polite, but she didn't care.

Rose was in an ultra-modern room, sleek as a sushi bar and cool as a glacier. The room was an icy sea-green, with a mottled marble floor buffed to a satiny shine. There was no visible light source, and the room was elegantly dim. In the center of the room was a seating... *thing* of some sort, shaped like the inside of an orchid and colored a deep purple—Rose had heard the color called "*aubergine,*" that meant "*eggplant,*" didn't it? Rose sensed a movement out of the corner of her eye, and whirled to see—mist?—curling on the floor. The room seemed to be in a tower. It was circular, and one entire wall curved out in floor-to-ceiling windows.

Rose was confused. There had been no tower on the brownstone.

And the brownstone was on a quiet tree-lined street, facing north, Rose was pretty sure. But these windows looked out on the lake, to the east, and all she saw out of them was water, far below, the watery horizon, with the—full? probably, it sure looked full—moon just rising above it glowing orange like a Halloween pumpkin.

Rose walked to the window and looked out. Where Lake Shore Drive should have been was a cliff-face, falling hundreds of feet to the water, raging white waves crashing against it far below.

Rose swayed a little and put her hand to the window.

"Rose, so good of you to come."

Rose whirled. Miss Van Lear stood in the center of the room. How had she come in? Rose hadn't heard the door... but there she was, tall, imposing, perfect, beautiful, looking regal in a scarlet gown, crimson in this sea-green room. Rose nearly bowed.

"Won't you sit down, dear?"

"This is such a lovely room, Miss Van Lear. I was just admiring—this view is amazing."

"Thank you, dear. I like it, too. It reminds me of home."

The two of them were seated now, on the aubergine thing. Rose realized the mist she had seen before was incense of some kind. It curled on the black-lacquered table between them, a sugary-sweet, sickish smell Rose couldn't identify. She felt a little dizzy, as if she'd stood up too fast, or maybe she was coming down with something. But this meeting was important, darn it, so she smiled. "It's such an honor to be invited to your home, Miss Van Lear."

"These little get-togethers are a tradition of mine; I think it's a good idea, don't you? I often like to have a little *tête-à-tête* with especially promising employees. And it's such a pleasure, getting to know each other a little better, sharing our ideas, our dreams."

"Dreams." A tiny warning bell went off in Rose's head, and she remembered the nightmares she'd been having lately. But no, it was probably nothing. Silly, really. She pushed the thought aside.

"Rose—you don't mind if I call you Rose, do you?—you must try a glass of this claret. I'd like your opinion. Let me know what you think. It's quite... old."

The bottle looked like it had been in someone's cellar for hundreds of years. Miss Van Lear's person was suddenly beside them, pouring the wine into two perfect crystal glasses. The wine glowed, a little—its bright scarlet redness in this cool, cool room made it look like it was glowing, and when Miss Van Lear raised her glass to her face, her face was lit from below with a smoky red glow. Odd, the wine perfectly matched her gown.

Rose sipped and was amazed. Wine wasn't supposed to do this—she was warmed, instantly, all the way down, and her heart slowed down and started to pound. This was some wine.

Miss Van Lear and the person both leaned forward, and were watching her closely, watching with great interest.

"How do you like it, dear?"

"It's very—I've never had anything like it." The room swayed a little, and Rose's heart, she could hear it now, thundered in her ears.

"I'm sure you haven't, dear." Rose leaned back, the wine and the incense were making her dizzy. The room tipped crazily, and the pounding in her ears became drums, huge drums, beating slowly in her head. Rose heard music, too, weird music, flutes, and someone singing words she couldn't understand.

Miss Van Lear's face was now the whole room, and each of her eyes was the moon, huge, each eye shining like the Halloween moon, riding the waves behind her.

"Your family and I have a history, dear." The voice was huge, too, and thrilling, like an organ with deep bass echoes, thrilling inside her.

Rose felt some alarm. She stood, saying, "I'm sorry, but I don't feel well. Perhaps I should just—"

The room tipped again. Miss Van Lear was now *below* her, somehow, below her, singing, with a slender black rod in her hand, like a magic wand, Rose thought. Then she saw the Halloween moon through the windows, riding over the waves, then Miss Van Lear again, then the moon, then Miss Van Lear, the moon, Miss Van Lear, faster and faster, blurring together. "Like a merry-go-round," Rose thought, and she giggled. "Wheeeee!!!"

Then the whirling stopped and she was whipped, shaken like a rag doll, whip-whip-whiplashed, and the floor came crashing up at her. The marble floor was hard and hurt her hands and feet when she landed, landed on all fours.

Miss Van Lear was now leaning over her, her face huge.

"I'm afraid you and yours have given me some trouble, my dear, and I never forget a debt. Now... you're mine."

Rose, still on all fours, craned her neck to look up at her.

In reply, she barked.

## CHAPTER SIXTEEN

# A Pewter Pin

Dear Alberta,

Oh, they're mine. You don't have to turn people into little white dogs to make them your slaves.

It was so easy: advertising. They have no defenses, no protections against images, addictive images, electronic crystal-meth that flickers at a frequency that matches their brainwaves. The images tell them they smell bad (who doesn't?) that they're not rich enough (who is?) and best of all, most soul-destroying of all, that they're not good enough.

Not good enough.

Once you get them believing that, they'll do anything you want.

And little machines they carry with them,
little machines with games, little machines
that pipe their own personal soundtrack into
their ears, so they never have to deal with
people. Little machines that give them
something somewhat like life. Little machines
that make them more alone.

So easy.
Why bother?

Oh, at first, I suppose, it was to get even.
To get even with the ones who made me believe
that I wasn't good enough. If I wasn't invited
to their party, I'd throw a bigger one, a
party so wonderful they would beg to get
invited to it, a party that would leave them
forever outside in the snow with their noses
pressed against the glass.

But... then what? Once you own the world, what
do you do with it?

My copy of the villain handbook was missing
that chapter.

So what now? More money, bigger parties? Or
move on to something more interesting?
And that would be what, exactly?

# The Hackers of Oz

Hmph. Irritating.
Makes me want to go kick some dogs.


xox,
Lyrissa


PS—On the ride to work today, there was a line
of tiny pre-schoolers, out for their morning
walk. Little kids in bowl haircuts and candy-
colored jackets, couldn't have been more than
five years old. Walking along in a line, holding
each other's hands, so nobody gets lost.

They used to sing, "Oh, we love the ooooold one"
as they marched. I didn't make them do that. I
think a couple of them might've actually meant
it. On my birthday, I got the usual suck-up
presents, but a couple of them seemed... one,
especially, a little pewter pin of a broom—
handmade, in a little box, not even signed...

Heck of a lot better than a skinned rabbit
from the kitchen.

Enough.
L

## CHAPTER SEVENTEEN

# Just the Band-Van

For a while, Elizabeth was fine. Her mom had been out late before. Elizabeth told herself that. She told herself that at 7:00, 8:00, 8:30, 8:45, 9:00, 9:10, 9:15, 9:17, and 9:18.

Rose had been out late before, but before, she'd always called.

Elizabeth tried her mom's work number, then the cell. No response, not even voicemail. Just, "ring... ring... ring... ring... ringggggg..."

Scraps tangoed in front of the TV. She had turned on a television show where famous people were trying to dance, and now she was gliding back and forth, imitating them with the sound turned off.

The Scarecrow sat beside Elizabeth on the couch. "I'm sure it's nothing to worry about," he lied, twisting burlap fingers together.

Elizabeth looked him in the eye. "You don't really think that, do you?"

"Was it that obvious?" He dropped some straw on the couch.

At 9:30, Elizabeth started to get ready for bed. Just a normal evening, she told herself. School tomorrow. Time for bed. Everything's fine. Certainly no reason to panic.

Elizabeth brushed her teeth, not thinking. She didn't think about robberies or kidnappings. And she really didn't think about car accidents. Instead, she brushed very thoroughly, paying attention to every tooth.

"You've been brushing your teeth for ten minutes," said Oscar, watching from the back of the toilet. "There won't be any enamel left."

Elizabeth thanked the bird, and went down to say goodnight.

"I'm going to bed now," she announced. "If—_when_ you hear mom's car drive up, come upstairs right away. She mustn't see you."

"We will." Elizabeth looked at the Scarecrow's worried face and wondered, how could a face painted on a feed sack be so expressive?

Scraps was still dancing. "Look, Betsy, this is the cha-cha!"

"That's nice, Scraps. Well, goodnight." Elizabeth stood there for another few seconds. "Listen, if..."

"What?"

"Nothing. Goodnight." Elizabeth went up to bed quickly. No sense worrying them.

She didn't want them to see her lip tremble.

She lay in bed and tossed. On one side of the bed, she saw her mother lying in a ditch by the road, the last words on her lips a whispered, "Betsy—no, Elizabe—*croak*." On the other side of her bed she saw herself as an orphan with hollow cheeks, wearing tattered Charles Dickens clothes, with her little bowl, "Please sir, may I have some… more?" On another side of the pillow, she saw herself at school and overheard the whispers— "That's Elizabeth. She lives on her own, very independent. I wish I could be like her." But the image that came up most was being held in her mother's arms, sitting next to her on the couch under a blanket, giggling together over some dumb movie. When Elizabeth thought about this, her throat got hot and tight, and the pillow got wet.

Then the room was light. Elizabeth must have gotten to sleep, because now it was morning. She jumped out of bed and ran down the hall, hurrying to her mom's bedroom, Rose had surely come home in the middle of the night, Elizabeth opened the door, knowing her mom would be there, getting ready for work—

The bed was smooth and unwrinkled.

Maybe her mom had already gotten up and was downstairs in the kitchen—but there were no coffee smells, and the house was silent, so Elizabeth walked, she didn't run down the hallway, didn't run to the kitchen door, and when she got there, and the kitchen was empty, and there was no mom in a ratty bathrobe looking at the paper, Elizabeth wasn't upset. She calmly walked to the garage door and looked into the garage, knowing what she would see: The pickup was still gone. The only thing in the garage was the band-van.

## CHAPTER EIGHTEEN

# Even More Focused
# Than Usual

*"A stuffy nose, a ticklish throat,*
*Some swollen toes, a nanny goat,*
*And that's the reason I called to say*
*That Betsy won't be in today."*
Scraps was on the phone, talking to Elizabeth's school. She listened for a moment. "Yes, nanny goat... N-A-N-N-Y...
*Why, no, I'd never pull your lague,*
*She's sick! She's got bubonic plague!"*
She listened again. "No, not always... Of course this is her mother! Who else would I be, the Patchwork Girl of Oz?... Thanks! You're very funny, too... Goodbye!"
She hung up. "Lying is fun!"

Elizabeth was even more focused then usual. First, she got a legal pad and sharpened seven number-two pencils. Then she sat down and made four lists. Then she showered, brushed her teeth, and had a nourishing, balanced breakfast. Then she brushed her teeth again. Then she called the police and the hospitals. After that, she brushed her teeth once more, then she packed her backpack: transit map, nutritious snacks, writing implements. Water. Sunscreen. A sweatshirt in case it got chilly. A compass. She picked up the pink plastic purse her mother had given her on her birthday that year. It had a beaded monkey face on it. Elizabeth considered it for a moment. "This is a little girl purse," she said to herself. "This is not a job for a little girl." She opened up the purse and counted—eighteen dollars and change. More than enough to get downtown and back, with a little left over. She folded it and put it in the pocket of her cargo shorts.

Scraps was dancing in the living room—"Look, Betsy! This is the Electric Slide!" The Scarecrow and Oscar sat on the couch, watching Elizabeth prepare.

"Where are you going?"

"I'm going to find my mom."

The Scarecrow's rumpled face turned serious. "Betsy, darling, you should just stay here, you don't know what's happened, you don't know where your mother is. This could be dangerous."

"I know."

"Are you sure you want to do this?"

"I'm sure."

"All right." The straw man and the bird shared a glance. The bird shrugged. The Scarecrow stood up. "Let's go."

Scraps stopped dancing. "Road Triiii-p!"

"No, thank you, Scarecrow," said Elizabeth as she handed him one of the lists. "I need you to stay here. There are many things I need you to check on. How are you with computers?"

"Young lady, you wound me." He raised one finger into the air. "You are looking at Oz's primary computer geek. Who do you think wrote the code that got us here?"

Elizabeth's eyebrows shot up. Uh-huh, she thought to herself. So that's how… "Good. All right. For now, I need you to go online, and check all the things on these lists. Sorry to give you so much to do, but it's important."

"Important! Excellent! I'll help!" said Scraps, dancing over to them. "You're asking the right person, I am very good at 'important!' Look! This is the Funky Chicken!"

The Scarecrow looked at her. "Um, Scraps, dear…"

Scraps flapped her elbows and whacked her knees to-gether. "I will be *so* helpful! Helpful is my middle name!"

"Um, well, these are pretty long lists. It's going to take me quite a while," said the Scarecrow. "Maybe it would be better if you went with Betsy."

"Nope, I'm staying here with you! I'm going to be *extreeemely* helpful! We'll get so much done! Look: Funky Chicken, Funky Chicken—maybe 'Funky Chicken' should be my middle name!"

Elizabeth and the Scarecrow shared a look. The Scarecrow put his hands behind his back and walked over to where Scraps was dancing. He cleared his throat. "No. Scraps, my darling, you have another essential function—"

Scraps kept dancing. "I have another essential function!"

"You must go into the city and look around—"

"I must go to the city and look around!"

"We need you to reconnoiter."

"I'm going to reconnoiter! What does that mean?"

"Look around."

"I'm going to reconnoiter!"

"It's essential for you to go undercover and learn all you can about this place—about where we are and how this world works."

"Undercover! How this world works! Essential! I can do that! Let's go!" She started towards the door.

"Um, just a minute." Elizabeth turned to the Scarecrow. "I don't think Chicago is ready for a walking, talking, patchwork quilt. She's a little conspicuous."

"Oh, that's not a problem at all," said the Scarecrow, waving his hand. "This is what we always do regarding that." He turned to Scraps.

Scraps put up her hands and started backing away. "No."

"Scraps, we've done this lots of times, it doesn't hurt a bit."

"Don't do it."

"If you'll just hold still…"

"Oh my goodness, is that a giraffe?" said Scraps, pointing up the stairs. When the Scarecrow turned to look, she ran into the kitchen.

The Scarecrow followed her. "Scraps, calm down, it's not—"

"Don't do it! It won't be necessary! I can be very inconspicuous!" Scraps, a multi-colored blur, dashed out of the kitchen and up the stairs.

The Scarecrow ran after her. He stopped on the stairs and turned to Elizabeth. "I don't know why she always makes such a fuss about this..." He ran up the stairs after her.

Elizabeth ran up the stairs too. Whatever this was, she wanted to see it.

The Scarecrow had Scraps cornered against the closet door at the end of the hallway. She shook one fist at him, "Straw man, don't you dare..."

The Scarecrow snapped his fingers, turned around, said some words, and pointed. There was a spray of plastic glitter and a smell of burning popcorn—"Noooooo!"—and Scraps shrank down to doll-size.

She crossed her arms and glared up at the Scarecrow from about a foot off the floor. "I hate it when you *belittle* me!"

Elizabeth didn't let Scraps see her smile. She picked up the squirming Patchwork Girl. "I know it sucks, Scraps. But that's how it's got to be." She turned to the Scarecrow. "Thanks." Elizabeth went down the stairs, grabbed her backpack, and tucked Scraps inside it, peeking out of the top like an angry patchwork papoose. "Let's go."

The Scarecrow stopped her at the door. "Betsy, one more thing. *Be careful.* Something tells me that we might be dealing with something very… important. Keep your eyes peeled."

"Thanks, Scarecrow." She hoisted the backpack onto her back and headed out the door. "I'm going to find my mom."

# CHAPTER NINETEEN

# 4308

*"Stand back! We've got no time to loiter!*
*Scraps is going to reconnoiter!*
*I'm sure that we will all agree*
*No one reconnoiters better than me!"*

The other riders on the Metra train looked up curiously over their morning papers. Elizabeth smiled a sweet-little-girl smile at them: "Ventriloquism." They went back to their papers.

Scraps pressed her nose against the window. "What's that? What's that?" "That's a car, Scraps." "Wow! Shiny! And what're those?" "Those are cars, too, Scraps." "Not so shiny." "Not so shiny, no." "What's that?" "That's a strip mall, Scraps." "Not so shiny, either." "No." "Is that a strip mall, too?" "Yes." "How about that?" "That, too." "There're a lot of these strip malls." "Yes, there are." Scraps whispered earnestly to herself, memorizing: *"Strip malls."* Elizabeth sighed. This was going to be a long day.

As Scraps went on—"Look! Another strip mall!"—

Elizabeth looked out the window and thought. She thought about her mom, and hoped she was okay. Rose had spent nights out before, but she'd always called. Elizabeth knew in her bones that this was different.

Different. In the last couple of days, her life had become *different*, all right. Suddenly she'd found herself in a *Twilight Zone* episode. Elizabeth had wanted her life to be different, but not <u>this</u> different. She gave Mr. Lefty Ring-Finger a couple of reassuring gnaws.

Scraps chatted on. "So where are we going? I'm undercover! It's my job to learn all we can about this world. Where are you taking me?" Suddenly Scraps stopped talking. Elizabeth was startled by the silence.

They could see the city now. The fall day was crisp and clear, and the city glistened, outlined in the morning sun. The towers and spires sparkled like Christmas ornaments, bright and fantastical in the morning light.

Scraps' face was pasted to the window, and her mouth was open. "Shiny."

"Yes, Scraps, it's shiny." The two of them were quiet for a moment.

The Patchwork Girl said quietly, "Oz is like that, sometimes."

Not so far from the Metra station, at the end of a street like a gray stone canyon, was the building where her mother worked. Elizabeth stood before it, Scraps' head poking out of her backpack. The building's front was granite, smooth and gray and windowless for several stories—just a wall of stone, but why did Elizabeth feel like she was being watched? She walked up the steps—there was a huge, old-fashioned clock face high up on the building, and above the doors was chiseled the word "Perfection." The doors were just doors, just like any other doors—why did they feel like a big mouth? Scraps, peeking out of the top of the backpack, felt it too. From inside the backpack came the muffled word, "Creepy."

The lobby was cold, polished gray marble. The reception desk was a large block of glass and brushed steel; a colorless young man in a gray sharkskin suit sat behind the desk. He looked like he was a part of it. Elizabeth walked up to the desk—even though it was just a desk, it made her feel small. "Excuse me?"

The man behind the desk pretended to smile. "Yes? Can I help you, little girl?"

"I'm here to see my mother, please."

The pretend smile evaporated. "Do you have an appointment?"

"Do I need one?"

His lips pursed. "Well, this is a place of business—"

"It's extremely important." The young man looked at her. Elizabeth looked back at him. She waited. The two of them waited, staring at each other. Finally—

"What's her name?"

"Rose Callahan."

The man's eyebrows shot up for a millisecond; then he recovered, and his face was once more as smooth as the marble of his desk.

"With a C or a K?"

"With a C."

The young man punched a few letters onto the screen in front of him. His eyes scrolled up and down the screen. "I don't see her—"

"C-a-l-l-a-h-a-n."

"Are you sure it's—"

"I know how to spell my name."

He frowned, slightly. "I'm sorry, I don't see her name anywhere. Are you sure you've got the right building?"

"Yes, I'm sure."

The young man pretended to look once more, then looked up at Betsy with a chilly little smirk. "There's no 'Rose Callahan' on the list. I'm sorry, little girl, but your mommy doesn't work here."

Elizabeth felt like she'd been slapped. The young man called, "Kyle, can you escort this young lady out?" Another young man in sharkskin glided towards her.

Elizabeth felt her face getting red, felt the heat at the roots of her hair, and she started to ball up her fists. She could hear Scraps whisper inside the backpack, "Easy, girl—take it easy. Just take a couple of deep breaths and—"

Elizabeth made a break for the elevators. On one of them, the door was just closing, and she dashed through it and heard the doors slide shut behind her, just before the young men—"Stop her!"—were able to catch up with her. Elizabeth listened to them pounding on the doors. She knew her mother worked on the forty-third floor—Rose had bragged about her corner office, and the view. She punched 43.

"Well, that was very exciting!" said Scraps, poking

her head out from inside the backpack. "What now?"

"I don't know, Scraps. We'll see." Elizabeth leaned against the wall, watching the numbers climb and feeling her muscles get tighter and tighter.

On 23, the doors slid open. A young lady in a sharkskin business suit carrying a clipboard stepped into the elevator. The young lady looked at Elizabeth briefly, then looked away without saying anything. Together, they watched the numbers. Elizabeth's heart pounded as she breathed out slowly. 34... 35... 36. The doors opened. The young lady got out. The doors closed.

Scraps asked again, "So what are you going to do?"

"My mom's office is 4308. I'm going to..."

38... 39... 40...

Elizabeth set her jaw. "I'll think of something."

41... 42... 43. The elevator stopped. The doors opened. No one was there waiting for her, just busy people in gray, working at their desks. Elizabeth stepped out. No one looked up.

A long hall stretched to the left and to the right.

Elizabeth guessed right.

Office number 4324, 4326, 4328—she was going the wrong way!

Calmly Elizabeth turned around and retraced her steps—4326, 4324—

The elevator doors opened. "There she is!"

Elizabeth ran.

4322, 4320—she ran down the hall. Three young men in sharkskin were pounding behind her—"Stop! Stop her!"

Elizabeth was on the track team. She was fast. 4314, 4312, 4310—she turned a corner—

And stopped. A man in gray overalls was scraping at the glass door of 4308 with a razor blade. Elizabeth could see where "C-a-l-l-" had been; the man was still scraping at "a-h-a-n." He turned to look at her and smiled. "Hello, little—"

"We'll take care of this." The young man from the reception desk stepped forward. Elizabeth thought to herself, he must work out. He wasn't even breathing hard. "Kyles, escort this young lady out." Elizabeth felt strong hands on both her shoulders, as two young men in sharkskin turned her towards the elevator.

She heard a deep, musical voice behind her. "Any problem, Kyle?"

"It's nothing, Miss Van Lear—" and Elizabeth turned to see Lyrissa Van Lear, the Perfect Lady, standing in front of a magnificent door at the end of the hallway. She was posed against the door like a movie star from the Forties, wearing a beautiful deep-green business suit that looked like a snake's skin, a suit that perfectly matched her eyes and the color of her nails.

When she saw Elizabeth, the Perfect Lady froze.

Their eyes met for a moment, and there was an electrical spark of, of what? Of—recognition?

Elizabeth's blood turned to ice.

"This way, miss." A firm hand on her back, and the Kyles "escorted" her onto the elevator. As the doors started to close, Elizabeth looked back. The Perfect Lady was still standing like a statue, clutching at the doorframe, the color drained from her face. She was staring at Elizabeth. She looked… frightened.

When the doors finally slid shut, Elizabeth realized she hadn't been breathing. Why? She didn't know.

But Scraps felt it, too. Elizabeth felt Scraps clutching at her through the backpack, huddled hard against her as they rode the elevator down. The Patchwork Girl was shaking.

*"Scary lady! Nightmary lady!*
*Beware-y, very afraid-y lady!*
*Definitely not hilarious.*
*Very, very, very, scarious."*

They sat on a bus-stop bench a block away from the Perfection building. The Kyles had practically thrown Elizabeth out of the building, and a security guard now stood at the door, watching, in case she tried to come back.

Elizabeth sat on the bench, her mind going like a hamster on a wheel. The name being scraped off the office door told her that her mother was in the building, or at least *had* been. But where was she now?

And Scraps would not stop talking. Once she had calmed down—why had they both been so frightened?—she kept asking Elizabeth, "What now, Betsy? What now?"

Elizabeth looked up at Perfection's huge, ornate clock. It was 10:30. What if her mother had just changed offices, and it hadn't gotten into the computer system yet? Not likely, but possible. Perfection was a big building, it was probably easy to get lost. Elizabeth knew if Rose was in there, she'd have to come out at the end of the day.

Which was five o'clock. Everything at Perfection was punctual, punctual, punctual, and her mother had made a remark once about Mussolini and trains that Elizabeth hadn't understood. But the end of the Perfect day was at five o'clock, when everyone who was in that building would walk out those doors. Elizabeth decided to wait.

"What are we going to do now, Betsy? What now?"

Elizabeth didn't answer.

"What now? What now? What now? What now? What now? What now?"

"Scraps, please. We're going to wait here until my mom comes out of those doors."

"You mean we're just going to *sit here*? But I have a mission! A function! I need to reconnoiter! Figure out how this world works! It's necessary! It's essential! It's vital! And *sitting here* is so *boooring*!

*C'mon, whatcha got, a goiter?*

*It's time for us to reconnoiter!*"

Five o'clock *was* a long time away. "Scraps, you're right. There's nothing we can do here for a while." She hoisted the backpack onto her shoulder, and adjusted it so Scraps' head was peeking out of a gap in the zippers at the top. "Now remember, don't let anyone see you move, you'll give somebody a heart attack."

They started walking.

"Where are we going?"

"You want to find out how this world works? I know just the place."

## CHAPTER TWENTY

# Reconnoitering

Elizabeth stood at the large, shell-shaped water fountain in Yesterday's Main Street, trying to scrub the chocolate syrup off of Scraps. "It's cold!" said Scraps. "Tough beans," said Elizabeth. Scraps splashed her. "Stop it," said Elizabeth. Scraps splashed her again, so Elizabeth held her head under the water for a long time, until she was completely soaked, and making gargling noises.

Elizabeth let go, and Scraps did a backstroke in the water for a minute. Then she got up and did a very respectable Gene Kelly from *Singin' in the Rain*. "MGM! Gotta love MGM!"

Elizabeth pulled her out of the water fountain and wrung her out. Scraps was very flat, for the second time that day. (A fat man had sat on her on the train.) Elizabeth held Scraps by one foot and whirled her around; the torque sent a shower of water droplets flying into the air. "Wheeee!"

"Let's go see if they have a dryer exhibit or something." A few minutes later, Elizabeth was holding Scraps by one foot under the jet-powered hand dryer in the ladies' room. Scraps waved under the dryer like a flag, struggling to hold her skirt down so people wouldn't see her patchwork underpants.

They had taken the Number 10 bus to The Museum of Science and Industry. Elizabeth knew where to go—when they'd first come to Barrington, Rose had talked about everything they'd see as soon as they had some time for sight-seeing. But Scraps was not behaving.

It had started with the trains. When they saw the huge model train set spread out over half a block of the museum's first floor, Scraps had leaped from Elizabeth's backpack, vaulted the plexiglass barrier, and run onto the exhibit. She stood beside a train track, just out of Elizabeth's reach, with her thumb out for a ride, holding her skirt up to show a little saucy patchwork ankle. When the train came by, she hopped on.

She waved as she rode the train through the paper-maché farms and villages, crowing:

*"Whoo-eee! Can't catch me!*
*I'm riding on this train for free!*
*Betsy-fretsy, so upset-sy,*
*Dullest Bets I've ever met-sy!"*

She stuck out her red velvet tongue at Elizabeth and did a little Charleston on top of the train.

"You'll have to get your dolly out of there, little girl." The museum guard was an older man with a silver moustache and a big comfortable stomach. He smiled at Elizabeth.

Elizabeth looked up at him—didn't he notice? Hadn't he just seen Scraps singing and dancing on the top of the train? "Glad to. Got any ideas?" said Elizabeth.

"Well, probably when she gets to the tunnel—"

When Scraps saw the train about to disappear into a cardboard mountain, she made a cartoon face and started dashing along the top of the train, running as hard as she could towards the caboose.

Not fast enough.

Splat.

There was a cottony, muffled sound and the security guard used an aluminum reacher-thing with a claw at the end of a long pole, to peel the Scraps-pancake off the side of the mountain. He handed her back to Elizabeth.

He leaned close and winked. "That's a very special dolly, little girl. You should hold onto her."

"Thank you, sir. I intend to."

Then he walked away, whistling softly to himself and smiling. The tune was familiar.

They'd looked at the other exhibits: the big beating heart that you could walk through—"I don't understand. Your chest is very small. How can such a big thing fit into—" The moon capsule, the submarine, the miniature fairy castle in the basement. Elizabeth had thought Scraps would feel right at home in the ornate palace, but she just turned up her nose. "Cute. Precious.

Twee. Trying way too hard," she sniffed. "Oz isn't like that at all."

The exhibit Scraps seemed the most interested in was the life-size "How Babies are Born" exhibit. She looked at it for a long time. "I'm a little confused."

"Most people are, Scraps."

"So how does this work, exactly? The baby grows in the mother's stomach? Isn't that uncomfortable? I don't understand."

Elizabeth did not want to have this conversation. "It's just biology, Scraps. You're not alone. Most people are pretty—"

"So the father plants a seed in the mother's stomach? How does he do that?"

"Um, biology, Scraps."

"Interesting."

"Yeah. Oh, look—here's the old-time street—"

"I have some more questions about biology."

"I'm sure you do. But look—here's an old-time ice cream parlor!"

…which is how Scraps ended up covered with chocolate syrup, taking a bath in the water fountain.

After the Museum of Science and Industry, they'd done The Field Museum—"Dinosaurs! Bony! Toothy! Scary! Roaaarrrr!"—and the Art Institute. Scraps kept Elizabeth in front of the Impressionist paintings for a long time—"No, don't move yet. Still looking." It was a painting of people relaxing on a Sunday afternoon done entirely in tiny dots of color. Scraps was quiet for

a while. "Oz is like this sometimes, too," she said. They walked on.

Through all their reconnoitering, Elizabeth kept her eye on her watch, and as it got later in the afternoon, she got quieter and quieter. Finally they started the walk from the Art Institute through downtown back towards Perfection. As they passed under the shrieking-steel corner turn of the L train, Scraps climbed halfway out of the backpack and held onto Elizabeth's collar so they could talk easier. A couple of people noticed the serious little girl with the funny-looking doll perched on her shoulder.

"I don't think much of your world, Bets."

"What?" Elizabeth was preoccupied. "What did you say?"

"I don't like your world. It's boring. Your world doesn't work."

"It's not so bad."

"Look around you—nobody's smiling. Nobody's singing, or whistling or dancing. No one says hello. What's the deal?"

"It's a city, you have to be careful."

"Of what?" Elizabeth had no answer. "And it's dull."

"How do you mean?"

"Well, is this all the colors you come in? You're all kind of *brown* aren't you? Pretty limited, if you ask me. See," and Scraps climbed a little higher on Elizabeth's shoulder, so she could illustrate, "look here." She pointed at one of the patches on her arm. "You're kind of pinky-brown—like this patch." She pointed at a man walking by in a hurry. "And he's kind of a nice Hershey-bar sort of color, like this patch. And there's a lot of shades of beige, and colors in between—but where's the blues, the greens, the oranges, the reds? This world is boring. I hate to have to say it, Bets, but you all look the same to me."

Elizabeth trudged on.

"This building is pretty," said Scraps. "What is it?"

"We can go inside. We've got a couple of minutes."

They entered the hushed silence, the smell of candles and incense, the afternoon sunlight coming through the windows painting bright-colored patterns on the stone—"Where are we?"

"It's a church, Scraps. People pray here."

"Wha??"

"People pray here. They talk to God."

"I don't see any telephones."

"No, you close your eyes, and talk to God—"

Scraps closed her eyes—"Hello, hello—" She waited for a bit. "He's not home, Betsy." She tried again. "And he doesn't seem to have voice mail. Or maybe he's got caller-ID and he's screening."

"No, it's not like—it's like you're talking to someone inside you, and you do it just by thinking."

Scraps closed her eyes and was silent for a moment. "Oh, there he is. Fine, and how are you? That's nice. The Scarecrow? He's fine, too. Betsy? Yes, she's very nice. You're right, she *does* worry too much. She's showing me the sights. Her mother didn't come home last night. We're reconnoitering. Well, I know you're busy—what? Why, thank you. That *would* be nice." And Scraps lifted up off of Elizabeth's shoulder and rose into the air, hovering just out of reach in a shaft of light. The stained glass added more colors to Scraps' already-crowded palette, and she floated there, spinning lazily in the light above Elizabeth's head like a gaudy, exotic orchid.

"Oz is like this, sometimes, too, Betsy," she said.

They stood on the corner outside Perfection, hoping that when the doors opened, Elizabeth's mother would come out. It had been a long day, and Elizabeth stared at the door, gnawing on one of the ties on her hoodie.

The doors opened, and her mom came out. She saw Elizabeth from the top of the stairs, and dropped her briefcase and waved, yelling "Betsy, Betsy! OOOO-ooooo!" She ran down the stairs in slow motion, and Elizabeth was a little embarrassed but mostly glad when her mother crushed her in her arms—"What are you doing here? How did you get here? It's so good to see you—"

Elizabeth imagined all the funny, tragic, heart-warming reunion scenes that would happen in a while. She hoped.

Finally, the enormous clock's hand hit twelve, and five tremendous bongs echoed up and down the street in front of Perfection. The work day ended, and the mouth-doors of the building opened, vomiting out a sea of gray-clothed, gray-faced people. As the waves of people poured past her, Elizabeth stood above them on a newspaper box, holding onto a lightpole, searching the crowd for her mother's face.

None of the people looked at her, none of their eyes met her eyes. Their eyes were either cast down, looking at the ground, or staring grimly ahead. The faces that made up the sea of workers were closed, like shut-up houses, doors and windows boarded over and nailed shut.

And not one of the faces was her mother's.

Elizabeth stood on the newspaper box for a long time, hoping. Maybe Rose had decided to work late. Maybe... but eventually the sea of workers slowed to a trickle, then a drip, then one or two. Elizabeth started to climb down. She knew it was time to give up.

A long, sleek beetle-colored limo pulled up in front of the building. Perfection's doors opened once more and Lyrissa Van Lear came out, leading a pack of little white dogs on leashes.

One of the dogs stopped and lifted up its nose, sniffing the air. It saw Betsy then, and leaped, nearly flew to the end of its leash, stood on its hind legs straining, barking at her frantically, high yipping barks, barking as if its heart would break, long, crying barks like screams.

One of the Kyles picked it up by its collar and tossed it into the limo. The door slammed shut. Elizabeth could see the dog pressed against the window, could hear the dog still barking, as the car pulled away.

No Mom. Elizabeth stood stock-still, wondering what to do next, as the street emptied around her. The afternoon sun had dropped behind the buildings, leaving the now-empty street in shadow. It was starting to get chilly. Elizabeth felt lost and alone. She sat down on a bus-stop bench.

"Well, I guess we'd better go home now," she said. She reached into her pocket. After all the bus fares and museum admissions, there would be just enough money to get home on—

Her pocket was empty.

Of course, she'd put the money in her other— "What's wrong?" said Scraps, as Elizabeth stood, setting the backpack down. That pocket was empty, too. So were all the rest of her pockets, as Elizabeth searched them again—"Betsy, what's wrong?"—and searched them all again.

Elizabeth turned the backpack inside out, and searched all the zippers, all the pockets. "Can I be of any help? What are you looking for? Look, here's a whistle, a compass…"

Finally, Elizabeth sat back down on the bus-stop bench with a thud. She had a horrible empty feeling in the pit of her stomach, and it wasn't just hunger.

It was fear. Elizabeth didn't know what to do.

"Here's a signal mirror. Is that any help?"

"No, Scraps, it's not much help."

"A roll of duct tape?"

"No."

"Well, what's wrong?"

"We're stuck here. It's getting dark, and we don't have the money to get home."

CHAPTER TWENTY-ONE

# Ride of the Valkyrie

Dear Alberta,

I'm writing this to you at the end of a perfect day.

The IPO—Initial Public Offering, the first day our stock was offered publicly—couldn't have gone better: standing on the podium in front of the stock exchange, and they handed me a gavel with a big pink ribbon on it! Well, I stood in front of them, ripped that ribbon off that hammer with my teeth, and slammed the gavel down like Thor's hammer, so hard that the podium cracked in two, right down the middle!

That's what I wanted to do. But instead, I smiled prettily and gave the gavel a dainty

little tap—the bell rang, and for a while we
all stood there and watched, as I became a
billionaire.

And they closed off the street in front of the
Perfection Building for a celebratory
luncheon: white linen buffet tables, ice stags
rearing in the air, liveried cater-waiters,
politicians and bigwigs balancing china plates
and champagne glasses, the key to the city,
the winged flutter of white-gloved hands
clapping.

For me.
All for me.
Little Lyrissa, happy at last.

And finally, this evening, after all the
waiting, after all the smiling and nodding and
being adored, finally alone. Alone, running up
the staircase no one knows, circling up stone
stairs, scarves flying behind me in a riot of
triumph, a riot of celebration as I fly up the
stairs to the top of the tower, a perfect onyx
circle high above the city, a perfect Autumn
night, the just-past-full moon (gibbous, a
gibbous moon) smiling down at me like a round-
faced, benevolent grandmother, as I look on
this city with—you know what's coming—with a
broom in my hand, and the tsunami of my joy

lifts me, and I rise, I jet into the sky,
straight, straight up, the wind icy against my
face, the one time I've allowed myself to be
airborne in this world, a perfect witch flying
against a perfect moon, and a Valkyrie cry
wings from my throat as I streak the night
sky, this little world, my little world,
spread out before me as perfect and as dear as
an impossibly expensive, unimaginably high-end
dollhouse. Soaring like the price of my IPO, I
laugh above this sleeping world; it's the
perfect end to a perfect day. Share my joy,
Alberta. Sometimes, not often, things turn out
our way.

There was a moment when I stopped, and hung in
the air over this adorable little world that
loves me so much, this world now sitting up
and begging like another little white dog.

Xox,
Lyrissa


PS—Alright, stop it, I can't hide anything
from you. I didn't tell you all of it:

"So what?"
"So what?" is what flashed through my mind as
I "hoy-yo-to-ho"-ed across the night sky. I

paused there, hung above my world, caught
between the moon and a large Midwestern city,
looking down at all that was mine, now. And I
thought, "So? You got what you wanted. Hoop-
tee-do. What now, missy?"

But, but, I argued with myself. Don't I get
to—can't I at least *enjoy* it for a *moment?*

"Meh. Sure. Whatever. Enjoy. Go nuts."

A couple more swoops against the stars.

Then the voice continued: "Now what?"

Well, I don't need to tell you, *that* took the
wind out of my britches. Triumph turned, not
exactly to ashes in my mouth, but maybe...
triumph turned to... I don't know, some
cardboard-y non-nutritive food-like snack
item of some kind, from the vending machine
at work.

Oh, fudge. Might as well go home.

And then the broom stalled. I turned it around
to go home, and the darn thing stopped. Just
hung there, a thousand feet above the
Merchandise Mart. Like it was tapping its
foot, if it had one.

# Ride of the Valkyrie

I yelled at it, of course, smacked it a couple
of times, and then it took off—but not
towards home, towards the *suburbs*, for Pete's
sake, *Palatine* or something. Well, I soon put
a stop to that—I took off my shoe and whacked
it, just kept whacking it with the heel until
it turned around and limped back home like it
was sulking.

Weird. Has that ever happened to you?

There's not a garage or something I can take
it to, is there?

Yours,
L

## CHAPTER TWENTY-TWO

# Hands

The new dog was crying again. Jervé hated this.

She was locked in the highest cage, huddled on herself in the corner, shaking, making sad little yips and whines and heartbreaking sighs. Her cage was four feet off the ground; even when Jervé stood on his hind legs, he couldn't reach up to her to give her a consoling lick.

Jervé had been disappointed: kennel life was nothing like *Lady and the Tramp*. There was no Peggy Lee singing doggie torch songs. There was no amusing cross-kennel banter, no Russian-wolfhound/British-bulldog dialect comedians. Because, of course, dogs can't talk. No, despite *101 Dalmatians*, the dogs didn't talk. Jervé felt like Uncle Walt had let him down.

Doggie language was rich, but it was mostly about what could be communicated through smells; most doggie greetings went along the lines of "gee, your butt smells terrific." When he'd first arrived, Jervé had tried to talk to the others, but, of course, his lips no longer worked, and his tongue was much too long. He could manage a decent "oooo" sound when he yawned, and of course a good "gr-r-r-r-r," but that was about it.

But the other dogs weren't much interested in talking. They'd been drones when they were human, and they were still drones—dull little worker-bees looking out for number one, just wanting to keep their heads down and stay out of trouble. Jervé tried to talk them into making a break for it, a lot of doggie charades and "rrr, Ruh Ruh, grrrrr, rrrrowlll… GRR!" (*"Rise up, oh my brothers! You have nothing to lose but your leashes!"*) But the other dogs just rolled over and went to sleep. There was no *Cinco de Mayo*, no doggy revolt brewing here. Just like in life, as long as they had cable and got fed on time, things were pretty much okay.

They were well treated. The basement kennel was clean, warm, well lit. Their day would begin at dawn, with her odd little *person* taking them all for walkies. She never said anything, just smiled her too-wide smile at them as she pressed her nose against their cages. Then she would open the cage doors, one by one, and snap their fabulous white leashes with "LVL" hand-burnished onto their collars, and out they would go, claws clicking on the sidewalks as they made their way to the park. People staring as each dog put down its own little baggie, flattened it carefully, and precisely pooped on it. "Man, those dogs are *trained!*"

Humiliating, pooping in public, but they were already dogs—how much worse could it get?

Then, riding to work in her espresso-colored limo, sitting quietly beside Her as She did the crossword. Now and then She would look over at them and smile at them like the accessories they were. And that's what they were, arm candy for She Who Must Be Obeyed, the perfect matching set, white dogs go with everything.

During the day, they would lounge on their doggie beds in her office. One of the newer Kyles would take them out for walkies. (The older Kyles, the ones who knew who they were, couldn't look at them, wouldn't come near.) Then they'd ride home, and get fed—dinner, TV and bed. Really, their lives hadn't changed that much.

Evenings, sometimes, after a few martinis, She would come down to the kennel and they would have to entertain. Jervé figured She was probably lonely—how much company could the person be? She would weave in front of the cages with a martini in her hand, breathing vodka on them, her face a horrible minty green in her nightly beauty mask. She would let them out and they would do tricks for Her, as She leaned, one elbow propped against a cage, watching them lip-sync to Motown girl groups and do chorus-line kicks to *"New York, New York."* Then She would get weepy, sitting on the floor with them gathered around Her, telling them sad, sad stories that always ended with a Good Little Girl and a bucket.

Then She would stagger out of the room, leaving them to climb back into their kennels and close the doors after them.

Jervé tried to tell himself that it wasn't so bad, really; but he didn't really believe it. Call it what you liked, a cage was a cage.

But everything changed when the new dog came. The new dog cried at night. The rest of them were numb by now, resigned to their lot. But the night she arrived, she lay in her kennel, whimpering to herself for hours. It took forever for her to finally cry herself to sleep.

And she tried to get away. The next morning, she tugged at her leash, then turned around quickly and *snapped* at the person, nipping a couple of fingers. The person looked at her for a moment, incredulous, sucking on her hand; then her face purpled with rage and she picked up the dog by the scruff of the neck and shook her till her teeth rattled. She opened her huge mouth and pulled back her lips uncovering dangerous-looking nasty yellow fangs. She bent her head towards the dog's neck—

"Nikko, that's enough. Behave." She Who Must Be Obeyed was standing inside the door. "Just put the leash on—she's new. She'll calm down soon enough." She looked at the new dog. "Won't you, Rose?"

At the sound of the name "Rose," all the fight went out of the new dog, and she dropped her head. Miserably, she allowed herself to be leashed.

Jervé did what he could to look out for her that day, show her the ropes, lighten her heart. He did what he could, but it wasn't much.

And tonight, she was crying again.

She Who Must staggered downstairs. Her face was flushed. Perhaps She'd been out in the wind or the cold. She had a shaker of martinis with a straw in it in one hand, and a broom in the other. She tapped the cages with the broom handle like a conductor tapping the music stand. "File out, rodents." They lined up before Her. All except for the new dog.

The new dog ignored her, staying in her cage. She was turned to the wall, crying softly to herself.

She Who Must walked over to the cage and stood in front of it, weaving a little. She leaned the broom against the cage. "Ha," She said. "Now you see. *Now.* Now you know. How it…" The new dog kept crying.

She Who Must watched her for a minute. "Oh,

stop," she said. "It's not that bad. Here, have a treat." She opened the plastic garbage can and dumped a handful of treats by the crying dog.

The new dog didn't move.

"Oh, com'ere." She picked up the dog and held it against her chest, petting it. "Iss not so bad. Iss not that bad, is it?"

Still holding the new dog, She plopped to the floor, carefully parking the martini shaker beside her. She stretched out one arm to the rest of them. "Com'ere, my sweet little doggies."

Oh, this was too much. Jervé bared his teeth in disgust. She looked at him, one eyebrow cocked. "Wha's your problem? Jervé, isn't it? Com'ere, rat-face." She reached across the floor towards the treat-bag, pulled out the bag and rattled it enticingly. "C'mon, don'tcha wanna a doggie treat?"

Jervé backed away growling, teeth bared. "Oooh, gettin' brave, are we? Showin' a li'l backbone? Baring your 'dorable little fangs?" She leaned toward him, breathing dizzying martini fumes on him. "Well, do your worst, rodent."

Jervé backed farther, not knowing what to do. Suddenly, a sound like a rifle shot went off beside him— "smack!" Jervé jumped, and turned, baring his teeth to bite— The broom was lying beside him on the floor. Had he knocked it over? Jervé was confused, he hadn't felt it. The broom lifted up a few inches and *smacked* the floor again. Jervé backed away from it, mouth hanging open. It *smacked* the floor once more, and then the broom jumped into his mouth. The broom was now in his teeth.

"Hey," She said. "Juss a minute. Thass not yours. Put it down. 'S not a doggie toy."

Jervé shook his head. The broom handle was wedged firmly in his mouth, he couldn't let it go. *It* had hold of *him*. He sank his teeth into it, shaking his head and backing away. The broom *thrummed* as he held it in his teeth, buzzing like he was biting down on a live wire.

"Give it here, rodent." She was starting to climb to her feet, sober now. She put the new dog back in her cage. "That's mine. Doesn't belong to you." She put out her hand. "I'm starting to get annoyed."

He backed away from Her, the broom in his mouth. The other dogs were frozen, staring at him.

"Now, rodent." She snapped her fingers at him, demanding. Jervé noticed that her hand was shaking a little.

Why did She care so much? What was happening? Was the broom something important? She seemed to care about it more than She should have—

"Now."

Jervé was about to make a decision, but he didn't get a chance. The broom made it for him.

It took off. The broom dashed out the door and up the stairs, dragging Jervé behind it.

"Stop him!" He heard Her behind him, screaming up the stairs. Which way? Footsteps pounded up the stairs from the cellar, and another set of feet, the *person*'s, was thundering down from the second floor. There was no time, which way should he go, he didn't know, he didn't have a chance to think. But he didn't need to—the broom yanked him around the corner into the hallway, dragging him down the hall into the kitchen.

Jervé looked behind him over his shoulder—the person stood in the kitchen doorway, roaring wordless sounds at him. She dived for him, but the broom in his mouth whipped him out of her reach and yanked him across the tiles to the doggie-door. Then it paused, thought for a second, abandoned Jervé, went back, and whacked the person half-a-dozen times on the top of her head: *whackwhackwhackwhackwhack!* A moment later, the broom was back in his mouth and Jervé was dragged to the doggie-door, then he was rocketed *through* it, into the back yard, into the night, to freedom. Behind him, the person's head thrust out through the little door, big teeth gnashing terribly. She roared at him again, one arm stretched out for him, fingers clawing the air, fist pounding the floor in frustration. But she was stuck—the doggie-door was too small for her, she was stuck in it, and she couldn't reach him. The broom still thrumming in his teeth, Jervé ran.

The kitchen door opened and light streamed into the back yard—She Who Must was silhouetted in the light—"Stop! Come back! Don't go!" Her voice wasn't just angry, there was a pleading sound in it that made Jervé wonder if She was really calling to him. But he didn't stay to find out, he ran across the backyard, past the garden with the pumpkins and last of the fall vegetables, to the garden gate that opened onto the alley. When he got there, the broom hammered the gate like a battering ram, again, again, again. The lock popped, the gate opened, and Jervé and the broom were through it and gone.

She stood in the light of the door for a long time, one hand on the doorframe, the other fingering the little pewter pin she wore. "Don't go," she said. "Come back." As the garden gate slammed shut, the pewter pin shattered in her hand. She looked down at the pieces. "Come back."

Jervé was gone into the night. The broom hummed in his mouth, louder and louder. It was hurting his teeth. He tried to drop it, but he couldn't. It really was like a live wire now, an electric wire that he couldn't let go of. The broom was dragging him, pulling him, lifting him off the ground, carrying him—to where?

Jervé didn't care. He was free.

He tried to open his jaws, tried to drop it. The broom began to glow, a weird green light coming off of it, intensely emerald, brighter and brighter, filling his eyes, blinding him as it *flew*, dragging him along wherever it was going. Then, he felt a painful, wrenching explosion throughout his body, pulling, stretching, tearing at him, ripping him apart, and then he was running *on two feet*, and stretched out before him, in front of his face, he was holding the broom in his—

HANDS!

CHAPTER TWENTY-THREE

# Lower Wacker Drive

Elizabeth didn't know. For the first time in her life she, Elizabeth Gale Callahan, had to admit something to herself: that *she didn't know* what to do. She didn't have a list, didn't have a timetable or a schedule, didn't have the usual, comfy rules and expectations that made life neat and tidy. She didn't have a clue what to do, she didn't have the slightest idea where to go. And the city was getting darker now; now it was starting to get cold.

So Elizabeth started walking, aimlessly, without direction, not knowing where she was going, just knowing it was a good idea to keep moving. They always told you, "Walk like you know where you're going, and maybe people will leave you alone."

With Scraps peeking out of her backpack, Elizabeth walked up the street to the river and out onto one of the hundred-year-old iron and concrete bridges that stretched across it. The sun was setting, a glorious smear of purple and scarlet and orange that painted the river

136

and the city around it a tawdry, majestic benediction the colors of popsicles and tropical fruits. Elizabeth and Scraps stood in the center of the river and looked at it for a while.

"Pretty."

"Uh-huh."

"Oz is like this, sometimes."

"Yeah, I guess." The two of them looked at the

beauty in silence. Then Elizabeth gulped out, "*I want my mom.*" Her shoulders shook, she put her head down on the railing of the bridge, and just let go. Elizabeth was alone, and Elizabeth was scared.

As she cried, Elizabeth felt small cotton hands patting her head, small cotton arms hugging her neck. She felt Scraps' head by her ear, and heard, "Don't worry, Betsy. We love you. We'll take care of you. If... if you need to, you can come and live with us." Elizabeth felt small cotton arms holding her very, very tight.

It helped. Some.

After a while, Elizabeth was able to breathe again. She hitched her backpack onto her shoulder and started walking again, slower now, with no real direction.

"So, what now?"

"I don't know, Scraps. Just keep walking, I guess."

At the end of the bridge was a concrete circular staircase with steel handrails, going down. They went down the stairs.

There was another level here—another street ran directly under the one beside the river; and there was a walkway at the riverside with cement benches and tables and chairs. Elizabeth sat down, and sat Scraps on the table beside her.

It was night now, and although the walkway by the river was well lit, it was empty and a little creepy. It's surprising how quickly the downtown of a big city can empty out at the end of the day. Now there were shadows. Now Elizabeth didn't feel so brave anymore. Or safe.

"What's the matter, Bets?"

"I—" Elizabeth didn't want Scraps to worry, she was worrying enough for the both of them. "I just think we should move someplace safer, someplace a little better lit."

"How come?"

"Well… not everybody in the city is nice, Scraps."

"Oh. Interesting. Well, maybe we'd better go, then."

They walked along the river on the street below the street. The mercury vapor lamps made the nighttime a sickly shadow-filled yellow-orange; the cavelike concrete walls shimmered with a green light reflected from the river. Everything here was concrete gray—the walls, the street, the walkway, the piles of discarded clothes—

One of the piles moved. Elizabeth saw that it wasn't just a pile of old blankets and rags—a homeless person was lying on the grating, wrapped in blankets, covered with a black umbrella to shut out the light.

And there were others—against the wall on this lower-level street, there was a row of men and women, even some children Elizabeth's age, camping out, sleeping on cardboard, wrapped in blankets. One or two looked up as she passed, but for the most part, their faces were as closed as those above ground had been. The faces Elizabeth had seen above ground had been closed in worry and resentment and fear; down here they were closed in hunger and tiredness and defeat.

"Are you lost, little girl?"

A friendly-faced black woman wrapped in a quilt was sitting on an inflatable mattress. She put down the paperback book she'd been reading in the light from the vapor lamps. "*Tale of Two Cities*. Some college kid started highlighting it, only got to page 32. 'It was the best of times, it was the worst of times.' You look hungry. Want some pad thai?"

Elizabeth did. "Sit down." The lady passed her a white cardboard container and a plastic fork. "Some nice young man dropped by the leftovers from his carry-out. I guess his date didn't go so well. Or maybe it did." She watched Elizabeth wolf down the bean sprouts, noodles and egg. Elizabeth thought it was the best food she'd ever tasted. She washed it down with water from a green Sprite bottle the lady handed her. "It's clean, I just filled it at the 7-Eleven."

The lady wore a blonde fro-wig and could have been any age from forty up. She pulled an old change purse out from somewhere inside her clothes. "Should we call your mama, so she doesn't worry?"

"My mother didn't come home."

"Oh."

The lady searched Elizabeth's eyes for a moment and saw the fear there. She squeezed Elizabeth's hand hard. "Don't worry, I'm sure she's all right. Are you warm enough?"

Elizabeth wasn't, and gladly wrapped herself in the packing blanket the lady offered her. "My name's Fay."

"Do you live down here?"

"Um-hm." She pointed to the people around her.

"Tale of two cities. Above and below, up the stairs and down, the haves and the have-nots. Down here, we're invisible—they don't really see us, don't really want to. But there isn't a 'have' above ground who isn't two paychecks and a hospital bill away from living right here beside me. Where do you live?"

"Barrington."

"You're a long way from home. You take the Metra in?"

"Uh-huh."

"Well, first thing tomorrow we'll get you back on it. For now, you just make yourself comfortable. That's a nice-looking dolly. Does she have a name?"

"Scraps."

Fay took Scraps for a moment and looked her in the face. The patchwork girl lay immobile in her hands, doing a great imitation of a rag doll. "She's kind of funny-looking, isn't she? Makes you want to laugh. Reminds me of something, from when I was a little girl…" She handed Scraps back.

"Funny-looking?" Scraps hissed. "Well, I never—"

"Shh."

"What's your name, little girl?"

"Elizabeth," she chomped out around a mouthful.

"Elizabeth! Well, that's my name, too. But my daddy always called me Fay." She sized Elizabeth up for a moment: the double knots on her shoelaces, the one gnawed fingernail, every button buttoned, every zipper zipped. As Elizabeth continued to wolf the pad thai, Fay said, "You know, Elizabeth, upstairs, everybody's holding on with all ten fingers, trying to *control* life. Like they can. It's like that baby on the cartoon, beeping the baby car-horn while somebody else drives. Life's gonna do what it's gonna do. Sometimes you just got to embrace the fact that you don't have the slightest idea what's going on, or what's gonna happen. Adjust, adapt, acclimatize. Sometimes, you just gotta let go and enjoy the ride. Wheee! What choice do you have?"

Next to her, Elizabeth heard Scraps whisper, "Wheeee!"

"Shhh!"

Someone was shouting. Fay turned her head—down the street a green glow lit the walls and ceiling of the underpass. It was moving toward them. "What the…?"

The shouting came closer. A man was running towards them, running down the walkway, fast, almost flying, crying, "Help! Help me!"

He was on fire—a green fire shimmered all around him. He held a broom in front of him in both hands, at times he would stumble, but he wouldn't fall—it seemed like the broom was dragging him. Between words, he would shout, noises that sounded like barking—"Help me! Help!"

Fay pulled Elizabeth closer to her. The green-glowing man was nearer now.

"Betsy!" Scraps whispered, "I think that might be—"

Elizabeth considered wildly. She remembered what the Scarecrow had told her—that she might find something *important*. Elizabeth had a *feeling*, about how crazy her life was now, about the kind of *story* her life had become, about the kind of choices living in a story like that demanded. Was this a smart choice? Was it appropriate? Was it wise? "Sometimes you just gotta let go and…"

Elizabeth stood up and stepped into the path of the burning man.

He was wearing a dog-collar and a leash. His face was twisted in pain. He seemed to be trying to push the broom away from him, but the broom wouldn't leave his hands. The broom dragged the man closer and closer to Elizabeth. It stopped in front of her.

"Help me!"

Elizabeth grabbed the broom with both hands and yanked. She ripped the broom out of his hands.

The green fire traveled up Elizabeth's arms. It didn't burn, it was cool, even somehow, welcoming, like minnows tickling in the ripples of a stream. The broom vibrated and hummed like it was electrified, turning in her hands like a huge, powerful magnet. As it twisted in the air before her, the fire dimmed and flickered. The green glow faded and snuffed out.

The man's shoulders sagged, and he collapsed. "Thank you," he sighed. He fell to his knees on the sidewalk.

"Thank you." He looked up at her, and licked her hand. Elizabeth was surprised—she didn't mind, for some reason it seemed natural for him. He was a youngish man in a torn sharkskin suit, with short-trimmed hair and horn-rims. Suddenly he stood, tugging at the dog-collar on his neck. He ripped it off, ran to the fence that separated them from the river, and hurled it out as far as he could.

"Jervé!" he cried to the city. His voice bounced off the buildings around them. "My name is Jervé, and *I walk on two legs!*"

Jervé turned. He was lost, lost in a universe of smells he'd never noticed before—the river, the night, and… pad thai?—especially the little girl who stood before him—a little girl with glasses and braces, a backpack and cargo shorts, a little girl who smelled like *potential*, like the fresh-washed air after a thunderstorm, when anything is possible.

Elizabeth looked at the broom in her hands. It was just an antique-looking old broom, straw and faded gray wood—but the handle was chewed. There were teeth marks, deep, like someone had been biting down hard on it. It thrummed again in her hands. She held it out to the man—

"Keep it," he said. "It led me to you, it was looking for you. *It wants you.*"

"But? It's just an old broom, with a couple of—"

"It doesn't matter," he said. "It's *Hers.*"

Jervé looked down at himself. He was relieved to see that he wasn't naked. Just like in the werewolf movies, when he changed back, his clothes had changed with him.

"How did you get here?" asked the little girl.

"Girlfriend, you wouldn't believe me if I told you." Jervé sat down and scratched behind his ear with his left foot. Then he bent over to lick—and was disappointed to find that he couldn't, anymore. He looked up at the little girl. "What's your name?"

"This is Elizabeth." A formidable-looking black woman in a blonde wig was standing beside the little girl. "She's stranded. Doesn't have the money to get home."

"Hmm," Jervé said. "How much do you need?" He reached into his pants pocket and found his wallet. He bent down, took some bills into his teeth, and pressed them into Elizabeth's hand. "Will that be enough?"

Elizabeth looked at the money in her hand. There had to be nearly a hundred dollars here. "Sure, but this is too much—"

"Keep it, keep it. You don't know how glad I—" then he stopped. "What—" he paused. "What month is this?"

"It's October. Why?"

"Oh." Jervé suddenly dropped to the ground again, sat down and hung his head. For some reason, Elizabeth wanted to scratch behind his ears. "What's the matter?" she asked.

Jervé looked up at her. Behind his horn-rims, his eyes were welling up. "I don't have anyplace to go. It's been months, I don't have a home anymore. Can I come home with you?"

CHAPTER TWENTY-FOUR

# Home Again, Home Again

Elizabeth was jazzed; she was vibrating with excitement and triumph. She'd made a choice, taken a chance, taken a risk, taken charge. Of course she wondered about this... odd young man sitting across the aisle from her. Of course she knew she shouldn't let a stranger into the house, but c'mon, all the rules were out the window now. She'd spent the day chaperoning a talking patchwork quilt. Her mom hadn't come home. There was a broom rubbing up against her leg like a cat, and an hour ago, she'd been juggling green fire. The rules were gone. Elizabeth was on her own now.

And she felt—powerful. Yes, she was worried about her mom. Yes, she didn't know what was going to happen next. But instead of feeling lost and afraid, she felt free, and powerful, and in charge. And it felt good. This would work out somehow. She'd make it work. What did she have to lose? Her life was as crazy as it could be, now—and it was exhilarating. She was jazzed.

# Home Again, Home Again

Thanks to the money in Jervé's pocket, they'd been able to catch the last train home. On their way to their seats, a fat man chewing on an unlit cigar looked at Elizabeth with the broom and said, "Why are you paying for the train, little girl? It's almost Halloween. Can't you just ride that thing home? Haw, haw, haw." He thought this was hilarious, and chortled to himself for a long time, repeating, "Can't you just ride it? Haw, haw, haw." Elizabeth gave him a microscopic smile.

In the bright lights of the train, Elizabeth studied the young man who was coming home with them. Short, sandy hair with dark roots, sticking up in places; horn-rimmed glasses that made him look like a grad student (or an accountant); gray sharkskin suit, worn and torn. Elizabeth thought to herself, where had she seen a suit like that?

The young man was quiet, looking out the window, looking at the nighttime streets sliding by. He seemed to be thinking about something. The whole trip back, he sat pressing his forehead against the window glass, as if he was trying to cool his thoughts down. He avoided meeting Elizabeth's eyes. She wondered what he'd left behind, what he was missing, what was lost.

"Want to talk about it?" she asked.

"Not really, if you don't mind. I've been… away. For a while."

"How long?"

"Hard to say. When you're eating dog food and watching reality TV, the days kind of run together." He looked out the window again.

Jervé was freaking out. His brain was on overload. He couldn't handle it. Everything smelled INCREDIBLY INTENSE. Every time he saw a squirrel or a cat, he had an overpowering urge to stand on his seat and point and yell really loud. Also, he was trying to figure out what he needed to do to put his life back together— did he still have a life? His phone didn't work anymore. Did he still have an apartment? Did he still have a bank account? God, his African violets hadn't been watered in how long? And when he looked over at the little girl—Elizabeth—when he looked at her, she looked back at him with clear, solemn little-girl eyes behind her glasses, waiting for him to tell her—what? He couldn't tell her where he'd been. It was all like some crazy nightmare now. And looking over at Elizabeth didn't make him feel any saner, either—the broom was rubbing her leg, and there was a patchwork doll poking out of her backpack playing peek-a-boo and sticking out her tongue at him. Jervé wondered, did the ASPCA take mental-health cases?

Also, he had to go walkies.

"You know, you'll feel better if you get it off you chest, whatever it is."

Jervé smiled a sad little smile. "If I told you, girlfriend, you would never, ever believe it."

"You'd be surprised what I could believe. I've gotten extremely good at believing unusual things lately."

The patchwork doll seemed to think this was pretty funny, and rolled around on the train seat, laughing and kicking her feet. Jervé looked back out the window, trying not to think. Ignoring the doll. And ignoring the broom, which had moved over and was rubbing against his knees now.

"Where the heck have you been? I've been worried sick! You're in a lot of trouble, young lady."

Elizabeth paused with her hand on the door. Part of her, the little girl part of her, hoped that when she opened the door Rose would be sitting on the couch with her arms crossed, trying to act furious, trying to hide her relief. But Elizabeth told herself not to expect it—there was no truck in the driveway, and she could see from the outside that the house was dark.

She told herself not to hope, but she couldn't help it.

But, of course, the house was quiet and empty when she opened the door.

She turned on the light and put down her backpack. Scraps clambered out of it and ran through the living room calling, "Scarecrow, Scarecrow! Where are you? Change me back! Change me back now, you animated haystack! I've reconnoitered! I've reconnoitered all over the place! I'm done reconnoitering! Turn me back, now!" Upstairs, the light from the computer screen in Elizabeth's bedroom was glowing dimly. Jervé stood inside the door, watching with an odd expression on his face as Scraps hoisted herself up the stairs one stair at a time.

Elizabeth turned to him. "I told you."

Jervé smiled, tight-lipped. He closed the door behind him, not letting go of the handle. He was glad to be able to hold on to something right now.

There was a "poof!"-y sound from upstairs, and he heard the doll say, "Finally!" The upstairs hall light turned on, and the Scarecrow from *The Wizard of Oz* came down the stairs, walked up to him, said "Hello," and put out his hand.

When he woke up, Jervé was lying on the couch with a damp cloth on his forehead, and the Scarecrow was leaning over him with a worried expression. The little girl's doll, much bigger now, was dancing in the middle of the living room. "One-two, cha-cha-cha."

"He's waking up," said the Scarecrow.

"I'm starving, do you want anything?" Elizabeth called from the kitchen. She came into the living room with a bowl of cereal in her hands. "I could make some eggs, if you like."

"Um, no, thanks. I'm fine." Jervé struggled to sit up.

"This is the Scarecrow, and you've already met Scraps." The grown-up doll waved to him, kicking her leg over her head like Chita Rivera.

"Don't introduce the bird. Bird's not important, everybody just ignore the bird," said the biggest crow he'd ever seen, perched on the back of the lazyboy, pecking at a fried chicken leg.

"I was getting to it," said Elizabeth, sitting down on the couch beside him. She waved her spoon at the crow. "That's Oscar."

"Pleased to meet you, I'm sure," said the bird.

"Um, the pleasure's mine," said Jervé. "Actually, I... I could eat something."

"There's more chicken," said the bird.

"Kitchen's in there, make yourself at home," said Elizabeth. Jervé left the room. She turned to the Scarecrow. "Any word from—any word about mom?"

The Scarecrow shook his head.

Elizabeth looked at her cereal for a moment. "I didn't think there would be."

"And your school called. They didn't believe you had bubonic plague."

"What a surprise."

"They expect you back tomorrow. Did you find out anything?"

Scraps cha-cha'd behind them. "We reconnoitered! We took a train ride! We saw museums! Betsy had pad thai!"

"We got that," said Elizabeth, tipping her head at the broom leaning beside the front door. "Jervé, um, gave it to me. It seems to be important. And it's very friendly. Did you find out anything online?"

"Well, yes I did." The Scarecrow puffed out his chest. "That URL you gave me was *very* interesting. Fortunately, I was able to… *do something*. Allow me to show you what I—"

"Tomorrow." Suddenly Elizabeth was *tired*. "Sorry, but I'm exhausted. Scraps walked me over every inch of Chicago."

"I was an expert reconnoiterer, wasn't I?" said the Patchwork Girl.

"You certainly were, Scraps," said Elizabeth as she took the cereal bowl back to the kitchen. Jervé was eating his chicken from a plate on the floor, while he and the bird discussed the merits of KFC vs. Popeye's.

"I'm going to bed. Goodnight." Elizabeth started dragging herself up the stairs.

"But I really think you should see what I've—" said the Scarecrow.

"Show me tomorrow. Too tired now. Going to sleep. Tomorrow's a school day." Elizabeth fell into bed. She was instantly asleep.

She hadn't even brushed her teeth.

## CHAPTER TWENTY-FIVE

# Colony Collapse Disorder

The next morning, after a nutritious breakfast and extremely thorough dental hygiene, Elizabeth went to school. Jervé had spent the night curled up on a blanket on the floor. When Elizabeth closed the front door, he was still asleep, twitching as he dreamed, like he was chasing something.

Just a few days till Halloween, Elizabeth thought, as she waited for the bus. It was a glorious fall day. The air was crisp and tart as a honeycrisp. The trees were outrageous, rust and fire-colors crackling against a faded denim sky. Elizabeth wished that her mom was there to share it. She felt a spear in her heart, of missing-her-mother-loneliness. Where was her mom? Would she... no, Elizabeth stopped herself. *When* would she, *how* would she... Elizabeth sighed.

Then the bus pulled up, and she got on.

"Glad you're feeling better, Elizabeth," said Mrs. Zimmerman, as she pulled away from the curb. "Better keep your head down. The natives are restless today."

They certainly were. The bus was a riot of noise— laughing and hooting and screaming, and missiles of all kinds flew through the air: somebody's homework, a soccer ball, even, it looked like, a turkey sandwich. Elizabeth couldn't believe it. This was quite a change from the silent tappity-tap of Internet chat. "Am I on the right bus?" she said, as she took a seat in the front. "What's up?"

"Search me, it's been like this all morning," said Mrs. Zimmerman. "Something in the water today? Bourbon, maybe?"

The ride to school was hilarious and chaotic, everyone having a loud, wonderful time, until the bus got to Penelope's corner. When the doors hissed open to let her on, suddenly the bus became hushed, then silent.

Everyone listened to the thumping dragging sound, as the little girl hauled her Nordstrom's bag up the steps behind her. Elizabeth gasped. The change was shocking.

Penelope was wearing her pink tutu, but part of it had come undone, and was dragging behind her, tattered and muddy. The satin toe shoes she clumped along in were stained and dirty, too. She wore torn, grubby sweatpants and a tee-shirt that might have been her father's, once. Her glasses had been repaired with a cartoon-character Band-Aid, her hair looked like a rat had slept in it, and the remnants of a pink tiara tilted to one side, half the rhinestones poked out and gone, looking like missing teeth. She sat down next to Elizabeth.

She smelled.

Elizabeth's heart broke.

"Hi, Elizabeth!" Penelope chirped. She reached into her shopping bag and brought out a fistful of slips of paper. They looked damp, like they had been chewed, or sucked-on. She dumped the wad into Elizabeth's lap. "Here! You should have these! It's great to be in a club!" Elizabeth looked down, and saw that the bag was full of them—all it contained was thousands of moist, crumpled slips of gray paper. Each one of them had the URL on it.

Mrs. McCumber looked at Penelope with sadness in her eyes, and with great kindness. She helped Penelope put her shopping bag away—"Here, dear, let's put this in your locker"—Elizabeth saw that the bag was torn. Behind Penelope in the hallway, and it had leaked a breadcrumb trail of little slips of soggy gray paper.

Penelope sat at her desk, put her earbuds in, and nodded for a while to the music. Then she got up and walked out of the room into the hallway, without asking. Mrs. McCumber followed her with her eyes, but didn't say anything. Penelope left her earbuds on the desk. Elizabeth reached over and picked one up, to see what she had been listening to so intently. There was nothing. They hadn't even been plugged in.

On the way to lunch, Mrs. McCumber asked her to stay. "Elizabeth, may I talk with you for a moment?" Elizabeth came back into the classroom. Mrs. McCumber stood by the window, sipping her tea and fingering the little gold watch pinned on her sweater. "Elizabeth, I can see you're upset. I am, too. Penelope was always such a..." and she trailed off for a moment. "It's no secret, her parents are talking about a special school. We're just letting her stay for a few days until things are worked out." She pulled her sweater closer, warming her hands on her mug of tea like they were chilled.

"Elizabeth, what happened on the playground?"

What could Elizabeth tell her? She hadn't really seen anything. There had just been the fog, and the kids in gray, appearing and disappearing like ghosts. And then Penelope, shattered on the pavement.

Elizabeth just shook her head. "I don't know, Mrs. McCumber. I wish I knew." There was no way to tell her, nothing to tell.

But now, everything was *different*. On the playground at lunch today, there was noise. There was running and shouting and kickball, and kids on the swings and the jungle gym and there was a touch-football game on the grass. Elizabeth was amazed. Something big had changed. What had happened?

And for some reason, there were a lot fewer kids in gray now. There were a couple, just wandering around listlessly—walking over here, standing for a minute, then walking over there. One or two would come together for a moment or two, then drift apart. They looked like they'd lost direction, like they didn't know where they were going, didn't know what to do anymore, like those vacuum cleaner robots when they run into a chair. Elizabeth actually saw one kid walk into a tree, repeatedly.

Elizabeth knew where she'd seen this before. In Minnesota, one of her friends had kept bees—his parents had a few hives, enough for gallons and gallons of honey at Christmastime. Last fall, one of the hives had caught whatever-that-horrible-thing-was that was killing honeybees, and their queen had died. Left alone, the drones had just wandered aimlessly. Eventually they died. That's how the gray kids were acting now.

Except for Ash. And Penelope. Ash had direction, Ash had a purpose. Elizabeth watched as he waddled from gray kid to gray kid, trying to herd them back into a group. One or two of them would follow him for a while, then they would lose interest again and drift away. As the lunch hour went on, he became more and more desperate, running from one end of the playground to the other, his sport coat growing a dark streak of sweat down the back. He couldn't keep them together, they just wandered off. A couple went to play football, a couple of the girls were on the swings. No one seemed interested in him anymore.

Except for Penelope. She followed him around, never far behind—followed him around in her muddy toe shoes with her torn, dirty pink tutu dragging on the ground behind her.

Finally, all of the gray kids had wandered off and Ash and Penelope were alone on the blacktop in the center of the playground. Ash noticed Elizabeth was watching him. He balled his fists and stomped over to her bench, red-faced and sweating. "You did this, didn't you?" he said quietly, leaning in close. "I know it was you—you had something to do with this. Well, we're not done yet. I'm not finished yet. This isn't over."

"Isn't over, isn't over, isn't over, isn't over," sang Penelope, dancing on her toes behind him.

Except it was, at least for now. The bell rang, cutting him off. Elizabeth picked up her lunchbox and went back inside, leaving Ash alone: a tubby, sweaty kid, sputtering on the playground, with Penelope, dancing around him, dirty, broken, and ruined.

## CHAPTER TWENTY-SIX

# Freezer-Burn

"Overload! Overload! TMI!"

"Give him some air!"

When Elizabeth opened the door, she heard a commotion coming from her bedroom. Scraps flew down the stairs into the kitchen, yelling, "Emergency! Emergency! Ice! Ice! Anything cold is nice, nice!"

Elizabeth ran upstairs. The Scarecrow was stretched out on the floor of her bedroom. His head was smoking: His hat was on the floor beside him, and two little tendrils of smoke were coming out of his painted-on ears. Jervé held his head on his lap, blowing on it and fanning it with a towel while Oscar flapped his wings helpfully.

"Oh my gosh! Is he okay?" said Elizabeth.

"Stand back! Scraps to the rescue!" Jervé got up and the Patchwork Girl dumped a bucket of ice onto the Scarecrow's head. From underneath the pile of ice came a muffled, "Thank you so much. That's better."

"What happened?" Elizabeth kneeled beside him.

"Temporary overload," said the pile of ice. "Nothing to be alarmed about. This is what happens when your brains are made of straw. The neurons overheat, the synapses start to smoke. If you don't shut down, your head could spontaneously combust. I had that happen at a party once, during a game of charades. Had to put my head in the punchbowl. Momentarily spectacular, but it made the children cry."

Scraps nodded. "And then you have to put his head in the dryer, on fluff. His head gets very big, so for a while he's *quite conceited*. But I usually put in a dryer sheet, so at least it smells nice."

"I'm starting to get soggy," said the pile of ice. The Scarecrow sat up.

"I have a better idea," said Elizabeth. "My mom does this when her knee is bothering her."

A few minutes later, the Scarecrow was sitting on Elizabeth's mattress with two bags of frozen peas duct-taped to his head. Scraps sat beside him, holding his hand. "Fetching chapeau," said the raven. "Very appetizing."

The Scarecrow ignored the snark. "Thanks! So how was school today, Elizabeth?"

Elizabeth sat down beside him. "Scarecrow, it was so weird! Everything is different now, I couldn't believe it! It's all changed!"

"I thought it might be," said the Scarecrow proudly. "Let me show you what I did."

"I learned an enormous amount yesterday!" The Scarecrow sat cross-legged on the floor, tapping at

Elizabeth's computer. "It would be a tremendous strain, of course, for most people, but for a superior brain like mine…"

Scraps rolled her eyes. "See? Conceited," she whispered.

The Scarecrow continued tapping. "Did you know there's a good deal of biology on the Internet? And everyone wants me to have a larger penis. What's a penis?"

"I know, I know!" said Scraps, sitting down beside him. "We saw some biology at the museum. It was very—"

Elizabeth changed the subject. "What did you find out? Anything useful?" She joined them on the floor.

"Oh, yes. Take a look at this." He scooted over, making room for her in front of the monitor.

He tapped a few letters and hit enter. He seems pretty much at home on the Internet, Elizabeth thought. Maybe his brain really is— "Here's the website, from the URL you gave me." Elizabeth leaned in and saw the familiar homepage. "Singing wildlife, dancing kitties, rainbows, unicorns, children with big eyes. All very harmless-looking. But perhaps you never noticed this: "He tapped a couple more taps, and the quiet music in the background grew louder. "Hear that? Sound familiar?"

Elizabeth leaned closer to the laptop, listening hard. It *did* sound familiar, a little. But mostly, it was… soothing. Comforting. Cozy and comfortable. Elizabeth felt like she was being wrapped in cotton batting, tucked into the biggest, fluffiest, softest quilt in the world, and all the problems with her mother's disappearance, and the gray kids at school, and the Oz folk in her bedroom seemed small now, small and getting smaller, getting far, far, far away—

"Stop!" cried Oscar. "Stop her!"

Elizabeth jolted awake. Scraps and the Scarecrow were looking at her, alarmed. "Did you see that, Scraps? Did you see?" The Scarecrow had turned off the website, and the two of them were leaning in close, with worried expressions on their faces.

"Creepy!" said Scraps.

"What happened? I just drifted off for a minute, didn't I?"

"Interesting," the Scarecrow said, his burlap lips pressed into a straight line. "No, you didn't just drift off, Bets. Your eyes turned white, and your head started to tick back and forth in time to the music, like a clockwork doll."

"It was creepy!" said Scraps again.

"Yes, it was extremely alarming," said the Scarecrow. "That didn't happen to me, but then, I'm not human. But it certainly happened to you."

"Yow." Elizabeth wondered if the website could be the cause of—

The Scarecrow went on. "And did you recognize the music?"

"Almost,' Elizabeth said, "but not quite. I think... I'm pretty sure I've heard it somewhere..."

"It's a marching song. The words are, 'Oh, we love... the Oooooold one!' They used it in the movie."

Elizabeth felt a chill go down her spine. Not knowing why, she looked over her shoulder. The broom she had brought back from the city was leaning innocently in the corner of the room beside the stuffed animals. It seemed—too casual, somehow. As if it was trying very hard to look like it wasn't listening. It gave her the creeps.

"How did this get up here? I left it downstairs. Just a minute." She carried the broom into the kitchen, where Jervé was mopping ice and cold water off the floor. When she put the broom into the closet with the cleaning supplies, it pushed against her hand, as if it didn't like being shut in the dark. Elizabeth closed the door and started back up the stairs. Then, she thought better of it. She returned to the closet and shoved a chair against it. As she turned to go up the stairs again, she heard a thumping against the door.

"So, Scarecrow," she said when she came back upstairs, "do you think the website is connected to the kids in gray at school, and—"

"It makes sense, doesn't it?"

"No. But nothing's made sense for a while, I'm getting used to it. But why was everything different at school today?"

The Scarecrow leapt to his feet and bowed, proudly. "Elementary, my dear Betsy! Everything is hackable. If I could get into the computers at the Pentagon..."

"Wait a minute, you got into the computers at the Pen—"

"A mistake, I was trying to order carryout for the bird." He sat down again. "But if I could get into those computers, getting into this website was a piece of cake. It was just a matter of…" He started to tap. "Let me show you what I did."

"You mean you already…?"

"Why do you think everything changed?" he answered. Elizabeth watched with interest. He *was* good at this. She saw pages flashing past on the screen like leaves in a strong wind. The longer he typed, the darker and simpler the images got, until they were just white writing against a dark gray backround. Then suddenly, with one final tap, everything stopped moving.

"Ta-da!" said the Scarecrow, presenting the new webpage to Elizabeth like a magician at the end of an impressive trick. "That's what I did. And that ought to do it!"

The screen was no longer a tasteful dark gray. Instead, the backround was a brightly colored patchwork. Against it, jujube-colored letters floated and danced:

"THis wEBsite IS CloSed BY OrDEr of hIS mAjESty, tHe ScARecrOw of Oz."

"And now I know why we're here," the Scarecrow went on. On the monitor, a picture of Al Gore popped up, thin and young. "The Internet hasn't been around that long. Back in the Eighties, Senator Gore was instrumental in passing the funding that created it. Look here." The picture of a young woman popped up.

Elizabeth thought she looked familiar, but it was hard to tell, her face was in shadow. "There was a young computer-science student at Cal Tech who was indispensable behind the scenes; she actually wrote a lot of the code that made it happen. And she carved her name into it, like someone putting their initials on a tree... it's on every Internet address, every time you sign on or go anywhere, as clear as..."

Suddenly Elizabeth smelled peas cooking. The Scarecrow's head was starting to smoke again. "Um, Scarecrow..." she pointed.

"Overload, overload! More frozen peas!" The Scarecrow ran downstairs to put his head in the freezer. Scraps ran after him.

Elizabeth moved to the keyboard. "What's he talking about? I don't see it... 'It's here, every time you sign on, as clear as...'" Elizabeth went to her favorite website, then another, then another. She looked at her browsing history, and saw:

www.huffpost.com

www.clevergirls.com

www.toosmartforyourbritches.com

www.investments.com

www.campingsupplies.com

www.practicalshoes.com

www.bigpinkfairyprincessdresses.com

"I don't see it," she shouted.

In the kitchen, the freezer door opened and more

ice hit the floor. "It's there, it's there, it's in every m-mmm-mm," the Scarecrow called back, but his voice was again muffled by a pile of ice cubes.

Elizabeth looked at the list. "Okay, what's the common... every address has '.com,' is that it? No, because some have '.org.' The underline? No. I don't... well, the only thing that's in all of them, is 'www.' 'Www?' Is that it? Every Web address has—" Elizabeth paused.

"We have 'www' in Oz, too," said the raven, discretely neatening his chest-feathers with his beak. "Means something different there."

"As clear as if she carved her name on a tree..." murmured Elizabeth. Suddenly, she had a terrible feeling. She turned to the bird. "It isn't 'world-wide-web,' is it?"

"Nope," said the bird.

"It's initials, isn't it?"

"Yup."

They said it together: "W.W.W. Wicked Witch of the West."

CHAPTER TWENTY-SEVEN

# The Broom

"Leave me alone, Scraps, I'm asleep."

Elizabeth didn't appreciate being poked awake; it had taken a long time for her to get to sleep that night. Another poke. She opened one eye. There was no one in her room.

Except for the broom, standing up by itself beside her mattress, not leaning against anything.

"I thought I left you in the—" she started. Then she remembered how her life had been lately: *Okay. No worries. It's perfectly consistent, hardly surprising at all that I'm having a conversation with a cleaning implement.* She sat up. "Yes?"

The broom bounced along the floor to the door of her bedroom, and then turned to see if she was following.

"Just a minute," she said. Elizabeth got up and pulled jeans and a jacket over her pajamas. The broom tapped against door frame. "I'm coming, I'm coming."

The broom led the way, hopping down the hallway.

Elizabeth followed. It was late, the house was dark. Light spilled from the door of her mother's room. The Scarecrow sat at her mom's desk, working earnestly on her computer. Elizabeth stopped just outside the door to the room—she could hear the Scarecrow tap-tap-tapping, gloved fingers patting away at the keyboard, "Hmm, more biology," he said to himself, looking at something on the screen. "Oh, c'mon, is that even possible?" Elizabeth held her breath, and tiptoed silently past the door. The Scarecrow didn't even look up.

Where was Scraps? Elizabeth thought. The Oz folk didn't need to sleep. What did they do in the middle of the night? Elizabeth tiptoed down the hall towards the living room.

The lights were on, and Scraps stood in the center of the room wearing headphones. She was practicing the Lambada. Not having any hips, she was finding it challenging. Elizabeth heard Scraps mutter to herself, "The forbidden dance of love..." and wondered what was rolling around in her padded cotton head.

Jervé was sleeping on the floor on top of a bunched-up quilt, twitching, with one of Elizabeth's old teddy bears beside him. It looked like it had been chewed-on. There was no sign of the bird.

Elizabeth saw her chance. She waited until Scraps did a particularly intricate move, and then silently slipped out the kitchen door into the house's tiny, green-plastic-coated-chain-link-fence-enclosed backyard.

It was a crisp fall night, clear, the smell of fallen leaves just beginning to scrunch the air. Elizabeth sat on the cement stoop outside her kitchen door, the broom in her lap.

It hummed in her hands like a live thing, vibrating subtly, almost purring. Elizabeth looked at it in the moonlight. An old-fashioned broom, obviously hand-made, it could have been a hundred years old. The handle was gray now, with fresh bite marks, and the rushes bound at the business end were dry and tattered as corn husks. When she stroked the handle, it thrummed with pleasure and rose a little, pushing against her hands.

"Well, how do we do this?" she asked.

The broom lifted off her lap and floated in the air before her.

It waited.

Elizabeth's mouth was cotton-dry. If she took the broom's invitation, what would happen? Where would it carry her? There wasn't a saddle or anything—what if she fell off?

The broom waggled impatiently.

Elizabeth knew that she had to do this. If she didn't, she knew she would regret it all her life, and die an old woman, wishing she'd had the courage. That was no way to live a life, she thought...

She stood, threw a leg over the broom and sat back, clutching the handle as tight as she could.

The broom rose about six inches. Elizabeth felt her feet leave the ground. The broom hovered, waiting.

"Okay," Elizabeth gulped. "Easy, now. Nothing fancy. Just once around the yard."

The broom hummed with pleasure, as if it was smiling. It did a slow, easy circle of the tiny backyard, practically turning in place.

Staying on was easier than she thought. The broom shifted beneath her like an old horse that wanted to make sure she was comfortable. They completed the circle, and the broom hovered once again, waiting.

"Well, it's late, and it's dark. There won't be anyone over by the school."

The broom rose gently into the air, and easily floated over the house next door towards the school, at a sane, tame, slow-bike-ride pace, about thirty feet in the air, just high enough to clear the roofs of the Barrington ranch houses. "Shouldn't we go a little higher? We don't want anyone to see—"

Thirty-five feet. Forty. Still floating gently along, a tiny breeze barely lifting Elizabeth's hair. She was no longer terrified, and now she felt a little ridiculous. How should she sit on this thing? She felt like a four-year-old riding a hobbyhorse, and wondered what the proper form should be. She seemed to be more comfortable bending her elbows and leaning into it a bit, with her bottom against the sweeping-part, for stability. Below her, she saw yards and rooftops, streetlights and empty streets, the occasional car making its way home.

Still the broom cantered easily along, waiting for her to relax. This seemed to be an old, patient broom.

"I suppose a little faster wouldn't hurt."

And as she leaned forward, the broom picked up speed, like a bike going downhill. Now she felt the wind in her hair and her eyes, bracing and chill. Beneath her, the streets clipped by a little faster, and Elizabeth found herself keeping pace with an SUV below her. Elizabeth smiled.

"Buzz it," she said.

And the broom dipped down like a colt finally given its head, and Elizabeth's feet tapped gently on the SUV's roof. Elizabeth pounded once or twice, and the car skidded to a stop. The window rolled down, and a man's head peered out. He saw Elizabeth, and his jaw dropped open. As they flew off, Elizabeth grinned and waved.

"All right. Never mind the school," Elizabeth said. "Let's go for a ride. Show me what you've got."

Finally! The broom shot into the sky like an arrow. Elizabeth leaned down now, her chest pressing against her hands. Ahead of her, stars glittered. Icy wind plastered her hair against her head, stinging her eyes, making them water. Elizabeth wished she had dressed warmer. It was cold up here.

And thrilling. And wonderful. And glorious.

They were headed towards the city, streaking across the night sky like a comet. Below her, the suburbs slept, tiny houses neatly laid out in tidy, safe, neat little rows. Before her was nothing but the star-filled universe, and now she was a part of it, high above the gray, boring, everyday world, the broom singing below her, the wind stinging her, whipping past.

The late Metra train was about to make its stop at the Barrington station. A fat man chewing on an unlit cigar dozed against a window. Elizabeth floated down beside the train, and tapped on the glass. The fat man opened his eyes and peered at her, half awake. He gave her a sleepy wave. Elizabeth pointed at the broom beneath her, and waved back. When he realized what she was riding on, his eyes bugged and he almost swallowed his cigar. "Haw, haw, haw," Elizabeth laughed, and rose into the air.

She had never felt so powerful, so alive. Elizabeth wondered if anyone saw a ten-year-old girl silhouetted against the October moon, and she threw back her head and laughed. Elizabeth thought about the drowsy masses snoring below her, dreaming their conventional, boring little dreams. She laughed at the timid, pathetic little people who would never feel what she was feeling now, would never know how powerful, how glorious it was to be —

The laugh that came out of her mouth sounded, well, *witchy*.

Witchy. Sort of like a cackle, really.

"Whoa," Elizabeth said.

Is that a part of the deal? If you ride on a broomstick against a Halloween sky, did that make you a —

"Whoa. Slow down."

But the broom ignored her. It raced on ahead, as if it hadn't heard. Ahead of them, the city glowed, giant toy blocks spread out against the orange, mercury-vapor-light glow.

"Slow down!" The broom didn't slow, didn't change direction, it rocketed through the sky. Where were they going? The broom seemed to know, seemed determined to take her to somewhere, where? Where was it taking her?

"STOP!" Elizabeth yelled, rocking back on the

broomstick, pulling hard, leaning back, pulling at the handle with all her might.

The broom didn't stop. Instead, it flew faster.

The wind was scorching Elizabeth's eyes now, banshee-shrieking in her ears. She turned her face away, hiding it from the wind, cramming her eyes shut and leaning into the handle. Elizabeth was afraid now, her heart going a mile a minute: She was being kidnapped. Where was the broom taking her?

To what?

Or to *whom*?

Elizabeth got mad. She was not going to be pushed around by a cleaning implement, even if it could fly. She shifted her weight, and, still holding on tight with one hand, reached the other frozen-fingered hand inside the pocket of her jacket and fished around. What did she have? What was in there? Duct tape, no, that wouldn't help. Several colors of markers, no good. Three-hole punch, no.

Wait—her hand closed on the indelible black Sharpie.

She pulled it out and leaned into the broom handle, taking off the cap. She felt really bad about this, but… She whispered into the handle. "Okay, cleaning implement. If you don't take me home right now, somebody's going to get *initialed*. Initialed, do you understand? Permanent, indelible, big black initials, all up and down… and my name is very long." Her brain worked feverishly, struggling to remember her class rosters from Minnesota. "Elizabeth, Mary-Francis, Mary-Margaret, Marianne, Mary-Catherine, Mary-Beth, Mary-Pat,

(Elizabeth had a lot of Catholic schoolmates) Mary-Martha, Mary-Diane, Mary-Aloysius…"

The air stopped whistling in her ears. The broom slowed.

"Mary-Heather, Mary-Candy, Mary-Brandy, Mary-Shaneekwa…"

The broom stopped.

"Home," Elizabeth ordered.

The broom turned around.

"And no more funny business."

The broom sulked towards the suburbs. Elizabeth hardly noticed the ride home; her mind was flying faster than the broom below her. Elizabeth had a lot to think about. What had just happened? She'd had a close call, and she knew it: The broom had almost taken her—where? Why? To whom?

These were the thoughts Elizabeth filled her head with to keep from thinking the thoughts that really bothered her, the thoughts she was trying to ignore. Not where she had almost gone, but who—or what—she'd had a taste of. That witchy laugh. Who—or what—she had almost *become*.

And what she had almost become wasn't what really bothered her, wasn't what made her gnaw Mr. Lefty-Ring-Finger to a wet, painful nub as she rode the sulking broomstick home.

What really bothered her was how much she'd enjoyed it.

How much she'd… wanted it.

## CHAPTER TWENTY-EIGHT

# Questions

The broom set her down in the back yard with a rude bump. Elizabeth took the broom handle in one hand, intending to march it straight to the broom closet, when—

"I was wondering when you'd try it."

Elizabeth jumped. She looked up. Oscar was perched on the edge of the roof. Poised against the night sky, looking down at her, the bird no longer looked like an overgrown crow. Now he looked like a raven: huge, sleek, glossy, and a little threatening.

"How was it?"

"Fun." Elizabeth had to be honest. "For a while. A lot of fun. You know."

Oscar flapped immense wings down to the ground beside her. "Not quite so unusual for me. But it's still fun for me, too, sometimes. I thought you'd like it. Well, goodnight." He flapped up to the top of the chain-link fence.

"Where are you going?"

"Little girl, never ask a raven…" Oscar tilted his head and looked at Elizabeth with one black, wicked little eye. "Ravens go raven places and do raven things. Just like little girls who ride broomsticks, do the kind of things that… little girls who ride broomsticks do. I might be going to surprise some rabbits. I might not." He flapped his wings three times and vanished into the night, black wings against the stars.

Elizabeth felt ridiculous lecturing a broom, banishing it to the broom closet for a time-out. So she didn't. She leaned it against a corner in the kitchen, pointing a finger at it and saying, "Behave." She opened the fridge and poured herself a glass of milk.

What Oscar said was bothering her: "Little girls who ride broomsticks…" What did "little girls who ride broomsticks" do?

Elizabeth thought about making some cocoa, but when she opened the cupboard and saw the little cast-iron pot, suddenly she didn't have the heart for it.

"Callahan women are resilient," she told herself. She bit her lip, and went into the living room. Jervé had woken up, and Scraps was teaching him the Lambada. "C'mon, you can shake your biology better than that," she encouraged. Elizabeth sat down on the couch and watched them for a while. Actually, Jervé could shake his biology pretty good. And Scraps didn't weigh very much, so she spent a good deal of time in the air. After a series of really impressive spins, the two of them reached out a hand for Elizabeth to join them.

"No thanks," she said.

"Don't be so gloomy, little lady! C'mon, shake it! said Jervé.

"Naw," said Elizabeth.

"Shake it like you're going to break it!" said Scraps.

Elizabeth didn't feel like explaining to them that she couldn't, didn't, never could, never was much of a dancer. She was too embarrassed to dance in front of people, she was so lousy at it. So, she never did. Instead she said, in a superior tone of voice, "Scraps, dancing is not always the answer."

Scraps whirled three times, leaped, spun above Jervé's head and ended in an improbably fabulous dip in his arms. "Betsy," she said very seriously, upside down with one arm over her head, "if dancing isn't the answer, you're asking the wrong questions."

Elizabeth looked at them for a moment. "Maybe," she said. She had other things on her mind. "G'night." She started up the stairs to her room. Jervé and Scraps watched her go, with worried expressions on their faces.

Elizabeth lay on her mattress, looking at the ceiling. What did "little girls who ride broomsticks" do?

Elizabeth sat up. Suddenly she knew.

She went to the trunk and got out the box with the wedding dress, the veil, the poppies, and the shoes.

She kicked her sneakers into the corner and stepped into the silver slippers. She didn't expect them to fit.

They did, perfectly.

"Take me to my mom," she said.

She started to click her heels together, but apparently, that was artistic license, too—

She was already there.

CHAPTER TWENTY-NINE

# Hello, Little Girl

She was Someplace Else. Elizabeth's eyes adjusted, and she looked around. In front of her, she saw water. In a dish. Elizabeth saw a dog's aluminum water bowl, inside a chrome steel cage with a rumpled terrycloth towel on the floor of it. The cage rested on top of a row of wire cages, nearly a dozen or so. Each one had a little white dog in it, lying on a rumpled towel with its head on it paws.

The dogs seemed to be homesick, or something. Some of the dogs were crying, whimpering themselves to sleep.

There was a shriek from beyond the closed door. "Shut up, rodents!"

Then, the door banged against the wall and the Perfect Lady stood silhouetted in the light. She was wearing a fluffy white bathrobe with "LVL" embroidered on it. Her hair was in curlers, and she had a blue-green beauty cream spread over her face that made her look like a Halloween witch. Her eyes were wild.

"Lyrissa's got a big day tomorrow, mutts, and she can't sleep with all that yowling!"

The dogs were instantly silent. All but one— Elizabeth heard one dog continuing to cry. It sounded very close. She looked around, but she couldn't see where the sound was coming from.

Then, the woman's face was huge and terrifying, blue-green, cracked and wrinkled, yellow teeth bared. "Shut up! Quit your whining, prairie rat!" Her voice was quiet then. "Just be thankful. There are worse things you could be than a little white dog."

Then the witch met her eyes.

"Why, hello, little girl."

Elizabeth froze.

"I see you." The blue-green face leaned in closer, and the vodka on her breath made Elizabeth choke. "I see you in there, little girl." She smiled then, and it wasn't pleasant. "I thought you might be visiting soon."

And she picked Elizabeth up in her hands and started to laugh, and the shock of her laughter threw Elizabeth back, yanking her like a bungee cord into—

Blackness.

Elizabeth was back in her room, lying on the sleeping bag. She sat up, and felt faint—she leaned against the wall for a minute, waiting for the terror to simmer down, waiting for her breath to come back.

Elizabeth didn't understand where her mom was, but she knew more now. She knew who the green-faced woman was.

She'd seen her yesterday in the Perfection building. Lyrissa Van Lear. The Perfect Lady.

And the last words Elizabeth heard the Perfect Lady say were, "I'll get you, my pretty! And your little *mom*, too!"

# CHAPTER THIRTY

# The Council

Suddenly Elizabeth couldn't be in a dark room anymore. She ran to the light switch and turned it on, then turned on the lamp on the floor beside her bed, then the light in the hallway. "Everybody up!" she shouted, running down the hallway, slapping her hand on the wall. "Wake up, everybody—Jervé, Scraps, is Oscar back?—we're having a meeting!"

The Scarecrow poked his head out of Elizabeth's mom's office. "I thought you were asleep—you had a big day, shouldn't you be getting some rest?"

"Stay right there, we're having a meeting." She yelled down the stairs, "Up here, everybody! I need everybody up here right now!"

Scraps sambaed up the stairs to Rose's office, followed by Jervé, yawning and rubbing sleep out of his eyes. Elizabeth opened the back door and called. Oscar, who'd been napping perched on the porch, awoke. "What's up?" he croaked. "A bird needs his beauty sleep."

"Come inside. I found mom." The raven flapped onto Elizabeth's arm—"Ow! Watch your claws!"—and together they went inside.

"It's very late, young lady," said the Scarecrow, once they were all together in Rose's office. "What's this all about?"

"I found mom. Or, at least, I think—I think I might know…" Elizabeth paused. How was she going to say this? "I think I know who has her."

She started to tell them what she'd seen, when suddenly she stopped and turned. She stepped outside the office. The broom was there again in the hallway, leaning against the wall beside the office door.

"Wait a minute." Elizabeth grabbed the broom and started to run it downstairs. It resisted her, pulling back, refusing to budge. "Look, I'm sorry," she said, muscleing the broom in a tug-of-war down the stairway, "but after what you did, I don't think I can trust—" The broom stopped resisting. "I think this will be better, just for now."

The broom paused for a moment, then flew out of her hands, flew down the stairs and rounded the corner into the kitchen. Elizabeth heard door of the broom closet slam. She winced. "Sorry," she called over her shoulder, starting back up the stairs. Why did she feel bad about this? Why was everybody so sensitive?

Elizabeth stopped short. What was she going to do? She didn't know. She wasn't prepared. She hadn't made any lists, didn't have a yellow legal pad to refer to, didn't have a single sharpened number-two pencil. What would her mother say about a situation like this? "Improvise, Betsy, improvise! We Callahan women are terrific under pressure!" Elizabeth took a deep breath and decided to wing it.

She walked into her mom's office. Everyone looked at her expectantly. "Okay, missy, what's all the excitement?" said Oscar. "What's all this about? What is this?"

Elizabeth said, "It's a war council."

As Elizabeth told them what she'd learned, she noticed Jervé getting more and more agitated. Sweat poured down his face as he sat on the daybed, twitching and making little noises as Elizabeth mentioned the dogs, and the cages, and the crying. Finally, when she got to green-faced lady, he started to whine. "Are you okay?" she asked.

"No, um, I... I think I... I think I have to go... walkies!" he said, running out of the room. Everyone was silent for a moment.

"Odd young man," said Scraps.

"High-strung," agreed the Scarecrow.

"Definitely in need of a chill pill," said the bird.

The Scarecrow looked confused. "They call her The Perfect Lady?' But her face is green. And you think this woman has your mother, somehow? Betsy, I have an extremely superior brain, but this does not... compute. It doesn't make much sense. You say she—"

"Um, I think, um, I may be able to be of some help here." Jervé was back inside the door, mopping his brow with a dishtowel and nibbling on a bone-shaped biscuit.

"I have some… experience with She Who Must, and I think perhaps I can fill in a few blanks."

He told them where he had been, before he met Elizabeth. Where he had been and *what* he had been.

As he finished his story, shaking and crying and sobbing into the dishtowel, all of them sat looking at him with their mouths open. Jervé went on. "And what did you say your mother's name was? Rose? That's what She Who Must called the newest dog, the one that came in a few days ago. Rose."

Silence.

*Long* silence.

"My mother is… *a dog*?" Elizabeth broke the silence. "This woman turned my mother into *a dog*… and she's keeping her in *a cage*?"

Elizabeth didn't look like a frightened ten-year-old-girl anymore. Now she looked dangerous. Angry, and larger, much larger. Like a tiger.

"Well, they're kennels, really, they're very nice, and it's only—"

"*Why would she do that?*"

"Hmm," said the Scarecrow holding up a finger.

"Yes?" Elizabeth whirled on him. "You have something to say?"

The Scarecrow leaned away from her, holding up his hands. "Well, um, it's starting to make a little more sense, now… if you think about the website, and the gray kids, and 'W.W.W.' and the 'Disturbance in the

Force' and, um… how *we* got here… and all that…"

"Yes. Yes. How you got here. Yes. Oz. Scarecrow. Scraps. Oscar. You haven't told me how you got here. It's about time. Spill it, straw man."

"Well… um," said the Scarecrow drumming his fingers on the side of his head for a moment. "How shall I put this?

"You know how, in Chekhov's play *The Three Sisters*, they're always saying, 'Oh, I want to go to Moscow, if only we were in Moscow, we'd be happy,' etcetera?"

"Um-hmm," said Elizabeth. Rose had played Masha in community theatre and hadn't been able to get a babysitter. Elizabeth had gotten to watch the play many times. She was losing her patience.

"Well, *Moscow isn't really that far.*" The Scarecrow folded his hands and smiled like he had just explained everything.

Elizabeth looked at him blankly.

"No, huh? Okay…" He tried again. "How about this: You see what you want to see, and you hear what you want to hear." Elizabeth looked at him, blanker. "Have you ever been to Dubuque? Have you ever been to Des Moines?" Elizabeth shook her head blankly. "You see? You see what you want to see, and you hear—"

Elizabeth launched herself like a rocket, shooting across the room at him. Suddenly her intense ten-year-old face was inches away from his.

"Okay, okay." He put his hands up again. "Okay. You know how you go to different worlds when you read a book? Or listen to music? Or see a movie? Well, there's a great deal of metaphysics involved, but basically, in the words 'alternate realities,' the important word isn't 'alternate,' it's *'realities.'* It's *all* real, every bit of it. Another way of saying it, is, 'if you can get to Oz by tornado, *it isn't that far away.'"*

Elizabeth's face was blank, blank, blank, blank, blank.

The Scarecrow sighed. "You see," he said, pointing to his straw-stuffed head, "it's all about perception. If you can *perceive* a world, see it and believe it, you're already *in* it in a way, aren't you? Already there? And if you're already *there*, why can't already *there* be already *here*, already? Or, as someone once said, 'East is East and West is West, and if you take cranberries and stew them like applesauce, it tastes a good deal more like prunes than rhubarb does.' I think it was one of your most famous philosophers, either Karl Marx or Groucho."

Elizabeth was suddenly sitting on top of the straw man, with her ten-year-old-little-girl fist inches away from his face.

"It's quite simple. Let me show you. Just takes a couple of minutes…" Elizabeth got off him, and the Scarecrow sat down at the computer. His gloved fingers started flying over the keyboard. Eventually he slowed down. He tapped a few taps, then a few more, and finally said, his finger poised above the *Enter* key, "Are you ready?"

"Do it," said Elizabeth.

He hit the key and all heck broke loose.

Suddenly a pissed-off ball of light the size of a softball was battering at Elizabeth's face, and the air was filled with a tinkling sound like a possessed toy piano with an incredibly vulgar vocabulary that consisted entirely of swearwords. Elizabeth felt her hair being pulled, and her glasses flying off her head. "Stop it! Stop!" she cried, trying to grab the glasses back. The ball of light swore at her some more, then books started flying at her off the bookshelf, and in the closet, all the clothes that had been on hangers were suddenly on the floor. Tinkerbell had grown older (and, um, put on a few ounces) but her temper hadn't improved at all.

The Scarecrow's hat flew out of the room into the toilet, as he typed and typed—"Get rid of her!" "I'm doing my best, but this part is a lot—" There was an *AWK!* and Oscar went flying down the hallway pursued by a furious ball of light holding on to his tail feathers like it was on water skis. Finally the Scarecrow finished: He typed '*Ctrl-Alt-Delete*' and Elizabeth's world rebooted. The explosion of tinkly swearwords was gone, and the air was blissfully peaceful.

"Hmm. She seemed a little upset. Perhaps we interrupted something," said the Scarecrow.

Elizabeth felt very calm. She fished her glasses off the jade plant. "That was interesting, thanks. Might be useful." She cleaned the fairy dust off her lenses with her tee-shirt. "But. I don't see how it's going to help us. We have to be able to…"

The Oz folk sat down to think. Jervé climbed out from under the daybed, where he'd dived when Tinkerbell erupted. The Scarecrow and Scraps held hands and watched as Elizabeth paced back and forth like a general in front of her troops. Oscar and Jervé shared part of a bone-shaped biscuit. Elizabeth marched out of the room for a moment, and came back with a yellow legal pad and a number of pencils, which she started to sharpen with a portable battery-powered sharpener.

"If only there was some way to *get to* her," she said as she sharpened. "*Get to* the Perfect Lady. But it's nearly impossible. She's extremely well-protected." She held up a pencil, looking at the point. It looked lethal.

"Protected? By what?" said the Scarecrow.

"Everything. Her job, her name, her..." she pointed. "Those guys in sharkskin, no offense, Jervé. People like that, people that big, are pretty insulated. It's like she's got a moat around her."

"I see," said the Scarecrow.

"It's mostly her money, I guess. She's got more money than Oprah."

"You can say that again. I used to have to balance her checkbook," said Jervé.

Elizabeth froze. "You what?"

"Balance her checkbook. Ugh. Horrible job, believe me. Woman cannot add to save her life."

"You used to balance her checkbook?"

"Ugh," Jervé shuddered. "Once a week, regular as clockwork. Took me all night."

"So... you have the password to her online banking?"

"Sure, why?"

"That's... convenient," said Elizabeth.

Elizabeth got an idea. An awful idea. Elizabeth got a wonderful, awful idea.

She thought to herself, are you a white hat or a black hat?

Are you a good witch or a bad witch?

She smiled then.

Then she smiled wider.

Elizabeth smiled an *extremely* wide smile and picked up the legal pad. "Okay, Friday is Halloween." She looked at the clock. "It's already Thursday morning. We've got a day to get everything ready."

"Here's what we're going to do…"

## CHAPTER THIRTY-ONE

# This Is Halloween,
# This Is Halloween

Early in the morning on Halloween:

Bad dreams again. That dream again: her street, the calliope music, that dot of color. She was headachy and hung-over and in a bad mood. She needed a treat.

Hm.

It *was* Halloween.

She went to her closet. Nothing, nothing, seen it before, the usual, the predictable, the mundane. Nothing worthy of her perfect specialness.

Of course there was...

Back in college, she'd tried on one of her snotty roommate's dresses—some huge pink chiffon number, with sequins and sparkles, big pink plastic-y crown. It made her look like a parade float. But... she'd sighed as she took it off and put it back. "Keep it," her roommate chirped. "I've got lots."

Well, she had kept it. Kept it in the back of her closet, never having the nerve to wear it, but now and then, evenings sometimes, she'd take it out and look at it, and sigh.

What the heck. She laughed. Perfect. This'll be a hoot.

Early in the morning on Halloween:

"No, you can't go with us."

"I know you want to, you can't."

"Because."

"Because I said so, that's why."

Jervé heard a voice in the kitchen. When he came around the corner in his costume, Elizabeth was already dressed, packed and ready to go. She was having a hushed, earnest conversation with the broom.

"You know the reason."

The broom, upright and floating a few inches off the ground, shook itself from side to side.

"Okay, if you really want to know… I don't know if I can trust you."

The broom threw itself back against the counter in outraged innocence and then laid its handle against Elizabeth's heart.

"Yes, I know you *say* that, but—"

"You know," Jervé said, "it's none of my business, but the broom led me to you. Like it was looking for you. Like it wanted you."

Elizabeth turned to him, hands on her hips. "Yes, it wanted me—but for what?"

The broom watched the conversation, turning from face to face.

Jervé shrugged. "I don't know."

The broom threw itself on the floor, its handle lying gently on Elizabeth's feet.

"Oh, get up. Fine, you can come, too. But I'm warning you, no funny business."

The broom rose up, and made a solemn "X" in the air.

"Cross your handle, huh?" Elizabeth looked at Jervé. "I guess that'll have to do."

The day before, they had spent all day making their preparations.

Elizabeth knew she'd need a costume, but nothing was right. Pirate, no. Witch, ironic but hugely inappropriate. But farther back in the closet, was an old costume Elizabeth had gotten as a hand-me-down from a cousin it had gotten too small for. Elizabeth had thanked her politely, and walked very slowly, had very carefully *not* run to her room to try on; she didn't want to show how thrilled she'd been. It was a genuine fairy-princess costume, with organza and tulle and sequins and sparkles, and a tall, sparkly transparent pink crown and a wand.

Elizabeth had loved it so much that she couldn't wear it. She couldn't show how much she loved it. It had to be private. She'd loved it too much to have people make fun of it, so that Halloween she'd just been a hobo again. Her mom had tried to get rid of it for the move, but Elizabeth had sneaked it back into a box, and here it was in her closet.

She'd never had the nerve to…

But Elizabeth's comfort zone had been demolished long, long ago. What the heck.

It had been… a little irritating when Jervé came back from the costume store, and she'd seen what he had picked out to wear. Jervé stood there in his costume: It was a pink fairy-princess costume, with a tall plastic hat, and organza, and sequins.

And he looked better in it than she did.

"Nice costume," she had said.

"I could say the same for you," he'd replied, snippily.

But now it was time. Scraps, Oscar, the Scarecrow and Jervé stood waiting in the kitchen like some tiny, crazy army waiting for the command from its general. Its general, who was wearing a fairy-princess costume and carrying a clipboard, a Macy's bag, and a backpack.

"Let's go," said Elizabeth. She tucked the backpack under her arm, and they went into the garage.

The broom followed, floating in the air behind them.

## CHAPTER THIRTY-TWO

# Latte

You didn't wear something like this to be inconspicuous. She *swept* into the Starbucks—"Good morning,
Miss Van Lear, good morning Miss Van Lear"—*swept*
magnificently, all organza, and tulle, and plastic-y
sparkles. When the crown almost got knocked off on the
door jamb, she recovered gracefully, with a *noblesse oblige*
smile. The drones getting their double-shot of enthusi-
asm parted before her like the Red Sea in front of Moses,
huddling against the walls, holding their scalding paper
cups out of the way of her gorgeousness. "Wonderful
costume, Miss Van Lear!" "Thank you, it *is* pretty special,
isn't it?" Always be gracious with the peasants.

She *swept* up, almost—well, not really swept, she
had to sidle, really, up to the counter, it was a *b-i-i-g*
dress (how did Glinda do it?)—and insisted on standing
in line just like a normal person. "Good morning, I'd like
a triple soy latte decaf espresso, with maple flavoring and
a dash of—" and then she heard the *rrrrrrip!* as the train

of the dress got caught in the door, biting off a chunk of her gorgeousness.

A beat.

Ha ha, these things happen, but the smile was gritted-teeth, and the air got chillier.

She handed the barista her bank card, and the register-peon, some spotty undergrad from one of the downtown colleges who obviously hadn't gotten up early enough to put on makeup, swiped the card and waited. Then she swiped it again. And chewed her gum. Then swiped it one more time. Then, "I'm sorry, Miss Van Lear, but there seems to be a problem with your card, it's been denied, in fact it says I'm supposed to confiscate—"

"Just give it here."

Immediately, there was a flurry of bills in the air, worker-bees trying to buy her coffee, and the panic-stricken manager comped her coffee for her, but on the way out, she heard a snicker, someone mumbled something and someone else laughed, then swallowed it, and Lyrissa Van Lear turned crimson, what the hell was this, was she *blushing*?

She thanked them graciously and took the coffee back to the limo and got in next to the dogs. "Shut it, rodents. Not a word." *Slamming* the car door... and catching. The train. Again.

She pretended not to notice. She wasn't going to open the door again. She could see out of the corner of her eye, inside the Starbucks, people were bent over, laughing behind the glass. Drive on.

Ohhhh, someone was going to pay for this.

CHAPTER THIRTY-THREE

# YMCA

Everything was under control. Elizabeth was good at this. Sure, their plan was crazy; sure, the stakes were desperate; sure, their adversary was as dangerous as she could be. But, she'd planned her plans and made her lists, and on the whole, Elizabeth felt okay. Except her dress itched her. And it was big. She kept having to push it down, sitting in the front of the band van, so she could review the checklist on the clipboard on her lap. Jervé seemed to be dealing with his much better— occasionally he'd wave at the traffic beside them, people pointing and smiling from their cars as they crawled together towards the city. Scraps and the Scarecrow rode together in the backseat: Scraps was picking out CDs and humming to herself, quiet for a change; the Scarecrow was tapping away on the laptop; Oscar had flown on ahead; the broom leaned against the back window. The back of the van was stacked with brown-paper lunch bags with "Cha-cha Bag" written on the side in crayon. They were as ready as they were going to be.

"I can't decide between 'Hernando's Hideaway' and 'Spanish Eyes.' What do you think, Bets?" Scraps teetered a stack of CDs on her lap.

"You're the expert, Scraps. Just make it something catchy." Then, the first sign that the day might not be a disaster, that they might have good luck: Jervé found a metered space around the corner from Perfection Street. As he began the docking maneuvers of parking the van, Elizabeth turned to the Scarecrow. "Are you ready?"

"Absolutely!"

"Alright then." She checked her watch. "You stay here, I'm going to send the signal."

And ten-year-old Elizabeth Gale Callahan climbed down from the van in her fairy-princess outfit. She walked over to the parking meter and pulled a couple of quarters out of her beaded monkey purse—the van would only be here a few minutes, fifty cents would probably be enough. Then she walked to the corner, winding up the duck. When the traffic light changed, she walked to the center of the street and released it.

A raven lit on a window-ledge high above the street and started to clean his tail feathers, casually, very nonchalant, everything's normal here, nothing to see, move it along, buddy.

Well, hello.

The street was a canyon of gray concrete: gray sidewalks, gray buildings, sheer rockface gray cement walls pocked with windows, a feeble gray light drifting down. Maybe someplace the sun was shining, but on this street, nobody would know about it for a long, long time.

She looked down from her window on the seventieth floor. Perfect world, perfect street. Everything muted, shades of gray, a tightly controlled color palette like winter, or the moon. Tasteful. Subdued. Perfect. Hers.

Usually this would have made her happy. Usually she would have stood there, looking down from her beautiful, tasteful office over her beautiful, tasteful street, contentedly sipping her latte watching the gray morning light sifting down like powdered sugar dusting the top of a wedding cake. What a world, what a world.

But today, she was… uneasy. Dissatisfied, or something. The dress had been a big success until it had been chomped by the door, and being dragged for several blocks from the limo hadn't improved it much. But it wasn't just the dress. The latte tasted funny. She was sure that girl hadn't mixed it right. And it wasn't hot. And the Kyles were late, where was everybody this morning? She was the only one there. And something was horribly wrong: When she went online to check her bank account, it said her balance was, actually said, "a measly two cents." That couldn't be right. What had happened? Surely that was a mistake. She'd find out as soon as the Kyles got in.

And that dream she'd had this morning was bothering her, gnawing at her.

So she looked out her window at the graying morning light.

Hm. A bird. This high up. That's... amazing...

No, it's not a bird. It's a butterfly. A monarch butterfly, hardly moving, just riding the currents of the air outside my window. Just one, this tiny little thing, all the way up here... amazing. Why are you up here all alone? Are you lost? Where's your flock, little butterfly? Floating on the air, right outside my—

Oh! What the—what is that? A *crow*? On my *windowsill*? Shoo! Shoo! Get away, you big stupid bird!

Oh! He made eye contact, I swear it, made eye contact with me *and held it* while he—Ugh! Yuck! How awful, you dirty, dirty bird! Ugh! I'll get one of the Kyles to clean that up, before it eats away the paint. Ugh.

Well, I mustn't let that *diseased* bird ruin my morning. Calm down, watch the side-streets beginning to trickle out my workers, streams emptying into the river of the little people who work for me, my minions—minions!—shuffling towards me in their Nikes and New Balances, balancing scalding, inferior coffee in cardboard cups with cardboard hand protectors not quite protecting their little cardboard hands.

How fast they're walking, how afraid they are to be late—hurry, worker-bees, hurry. Don't want to be late. That's it, run.


The Perfect Lady didn't see the abnormality, the flaw, the blemish at the end of her street. Barely visible at the end of the street was something tiny and shiny and brightly colored. She surely wouldn't have been able to see it from her window high above, wouldn't have been able to tell what it was that was rolling down the end of her street towards Perfection. But even if she could have seen it, she probably wouldn't have had an inkling that she was looking at her doom:

It was a wind-up toy of a quacking duck riding a tricycle. As the duck's feet pedaled the tricycle, the propeller on its beanie whirled. It moved down the street towards Perfection, pedaling its tricycle and quacking. In the midst of the tasteful gray world that was Perfection, the duck was noisy and garish and ridiculous.

Pedal, pedal, pedal. Quack, quack, quack.

Nice ledge. Spacious, accommodating. And the look on the old bat's face when I showed her what I really thought—priceless.

Oscar watched from the window ledge, taking in, from high above, the bird's-eye view: a bunch of humans hopping around. Thousands of years of plagues, crusades, political campaigns, and wars: a bunch of humans getting excited, hopping around. Here, it was a street full of people dressed in business suits, worrying their way towards this pile of rocks, where they'll work until they croak. Great idea. He took another satisfying dump.

So, where's the duck? I'm not seeing—oh, there it is. Okay, a tail feather, pick a sturdy one—yow! *That* smarts! With the feather in his beak, Oscar glided off the ledge, down towards the clock.

On this street, it was impossible not to know what time it was. Perfection's perfect clock face dominated the street. The clock's perfect dial was nine feet wide, and handmade of ecru Italian frosted glass. The time was told in Roman numerals, and the clock's hands were ornately hand-crafted in the serpentine style.

The clock was superb, the masterpiece of an old-world clockmaker's art: Its hands were attached to the clock's *motion* by the *retaining pin*, which passed through the *centre arbor*; the hands affixed by the *hand collet* onto the *minute pipe*, which turned within the *hour wheel*. A hundred years ago, a *pendulum* would have powered the *escapement*, the *minute spring* powering the *cannon wheel*, which turned the *hour* and *minute wheels*. These days, it was all electronic, synchronized with the *cesium atomic clocks* and *hydrogen maser clocks* of the *U.S. Naval Observatory's mean timescale* to a variance of less than seven *picoseconds* per day.

Whatever.

The raven wedged a tail feather into the clockface just above the second hand, and the darn thing stopped.

Gray faces, downcast eyes, silent except for the occasional mumbled "excuse me," the masses of the enslaved shuffled toward Perfection without joy. Smart briefcases bruised their knees, coffee cooked their knuckles, worry haunted their eyes and the corners of their mouths and made little wrinkles between their eyebrows they'd spend a lot of money later trying to erase. There was no flirting, there were no jokes, no "doing anything this weekend?" Just the sound of running shoes scuffling on concrete. Now and then each would glance at the magnificent clock above them, each knowing exactly how many seconds it took to get to their desk, each mentally computing whether they needed to walk faster, jog, or start running.

The slaves that built the pyramids were happier.

No one had figured out yet that the clock was stopped.

Joanne Rosenbush trudged towards Perfection. She'd found out after her retirement that her kindergarten teacher's pension just covered the bills, her mortgage, and her car payment, and she'd gotten bored playing computer solitaire and watching daytime television, so she'd taken a copywriter's job at Perfection. The only other jobs open to her in this economy required paper hats.

She trudged towards Perfection in her little gray suit. Amazing how rigid an unspoken rule could be. In her bag was her floppy red hat, the hat that told the world that she was still a fun old broad and a force to be reckoned with. Each morning, before she got to Perfection, she took it off. When she was at Perfection, she kept it in her bag. At Perfection, nobody cared who she was.

She trudged towards Perfection counting the gum spots on the sidewalk, the gray pants and skirts around her entombing her in gray wool. She knew she was going to work until she died. Or work until she was incapable of working any more and then died. Or until she shot somebody, was sent to prison and then died. This idea gave her hope.

The river of workers slowed a bit, and there was a little white water, as workers looked up at the clock and saw... that they had a little more time than they'd thought. They stopped running, most of them, and relaxed a little. Some of them wondered if they had time for a doughnut. A few of them stopped for a paper. Joanne Rosenbush stopped to look up at the sky far above her, a faraway promise of sunlit blue book-ended by walls of stone.

Calliope music. What? *Calliope music* broke her reverie. This was annoying, she hadn't noticed the sky in, how long? And now this noise was—she turned, looking as if she was going to scold someone. Then she laughed.

It was ridiculous. There was a twenty-year-old brown conversion van inching down the middle of the street, blaring bad cha-cha music. The side of the van said "Pussy Pirates," with a semi-professionally air-brushed illustration of cats in eyepatches. On top of the van, a woman in a hilarious patchwork clown costume—it *was* Halloween, wasn't it?—was holding a microphone.

"Good morning, everybody! Time for your morning cha-cha lesson!" The van stopped and music started—the Herb Alpert 'Spanish Eyes'—and the lady in patchwork chirped at them, "Now say it with me, one, two, cha-cha-cha—"

This was ridiculous. Another something rippled

through the river of workers—here and there some eyes met, here and there somebody smiled a little. Many of them checked the clock—still plenty of time—and stopped to watch the show. The patchwork lady was demonstrating: "Come on, people, you've all got *biology*, I want to see you shake it—one, two, cha-cha-cha—"

Not just smiles, now, grins, and here and there, some of them stopped in their march to Perfection and did an apologetic little cha-cha, and then laughed, half-embarrassed at themselves for their silliness.

"May I have this dance?" A man dressed as a scarecrow danced in front of her, a crazy smile painted on his face.

Joanne remembered who she was—remembered that she was a fun person, with a nutty sense of humor, and that she'd swung a mean cha-cha when she was younger. "Of course." She took the scarecrow's hands— How did they do that? It really felt like there was straw in his gloves, not fingers—and they started to dance.

Joanne noticed that he even smelled like straw—the sweet, dusty smell she hadn't smelled for—was it fifty years?—must be—since she was a little girl, visiting her Uncle Bud and Aunt Genevieve's farm when she was ten. She breathed in the smell: of clover, and August and summer vacation with weeks of blessed freedom before having to go back to school.

Joanne and the Scarecrow danced. Seriously. So seriously, it was hard not to laugh. So seriously, they did laugh.

And Joanne remembered—dances as a girl, sock

hops, and boys, and how good it was to shake your "biology" with a man in your arms—and she got a little angry—angry at herself for forgetting this, angry at the world, at her job, for letting her—making her—forget it.

And she remembered the red hat at the bottom of her bag—the hat she'd bought last summer, the hat that told the world, "Hey, I'm no spring chicken, but I'm still a hot tamale!" And she pulled it out of her bag, shook it out, and put it on, defiantly.

An attractive older gentleman with a comb-over tapped the Scarecrow on the shoulder—"May I cut in?" The Scarecrow bowed and stepped away, and Joanne looked into the twinkling eyes of Arthur Portscheller, who worked in accounting. He winked at her and said, "Nice hat."

"Okay, everybody! YMCA!"

The Patchwork Girl led the dancing from the top of the van. The mood on the street was completely changed. People were dancing—no, *everyone* was dancing: middle-aged worker-bees sweating to the oldies, women in Nikes and business suits, fat guys wiping the sweat off their glasses, and everyone was smiling— in fact, most of them were laughing, as they chanted "Y-M-C-A! Y-M-C-A!" Buttoned-down young men in sharkskin with too-tight pants were the best at it—in fact, there was a whole group of them dancing together very well; some of them even took their shirts off. Briefcases opened, and the street was showered with, it looked like, extremely important business papers. No one seemed to care. All over the street, ties were loosened. Glasses came off. Collars were undone. Hair came down.

Scraps encouraged the dancers— "It's a beautiful day! Haven't you got something better to do than *work*? And someone better to do it with? Wouldn't today be a great day to _call in sick?_ "—and hundreds of dancers fished out their cell phones and the phone lines of Perfection lit up. The Scarecrow was back in the van by now, and Elizabeth cued him from the shotgun seat— "Now!" He opened up the laptop and typed for several minutes, then started hitting *Enter! Enter! Enter!* The van's back doors flew open and Elizabeth could just see in the rear-view mirror a flash of light and something— silver? aluminum? tin?—then another flash, and something big and hairy and tawny-colored, with a Bronx dialect and a lion's roar...

And soon, the worker-bees were only half of the dance floor crowding the street in front of Perfection— the other half was *odder*. There was a ball-shaped mechanical man with a derby and glasses. There was a man with a pumpkin for a head dancing with a sawhorse. There was a bolted-together pair of loveseats with a goat's head on the end of it. There was a big bug in a top hat dancing on its hind legs; there were dancing dolls of porcelain, an unusual number of short people, and a talking chicken; and over it all hovered a big pink bubble, with a nice-looking older lady inside it. And there were people of all colors—*all* colors—green, and yellow and blue, not just monotonous beiges and browns. The worker-bees danced with the Ozzites, without question—it was Halloween, wasn't it?—with an "I'm-already-late-for-work–what-the-heck" kind of celebration. Some of the office boys showed the Ozzites how to spin on a piece of cardboard on the ground; some of the worker-bees taught the Ozzites the Electric Slide. The Electric Slide is, of course, universal and irresistible. Finally the whole street was doing the Electric Slide towards Perfection.

Watching, from the window on the seventieth floor: What the heck is going on? What's happening?

Don't you know you're going to be *late?* Doesn't that make you afraid? It should! Stop dancing, all of you! I'm not paying you to dance!

GET IN HERE!

She pressed a button on her desk and waited a minute, *two* minutes. "I'm *waiting...*" she called. Usually those words caused a panicked spasm of activity, but *nothing was happening.* She could hear phones ringing all over the building as all over the building messages were being left: worker-bees calling in late for work, or even—outrageous!—*calling in sick.*

She had to put a stop to this. She put on the pink plastic crown, pulled her enormous dress around her, swept into the elevator and pressed "Lobby."

The Scarecrow hunched over the laptop, punching furiously. He said "poot!" occasionally, and sometimes, "drat!" As he typed, his straw fingers occasionally hit two keys at once, and he had to delete, and go back—

"Scarecrow, it's time!" Elizabeth looked back at him from the front seat.

"I know, I know, I'm typing as fast as I—"

And the street around them changed.

Suddenly, it was winter. Every surface of the street was suddenly covered with snow and ice, and snowflakes filled the air. It had happened so quickly—in the blink of an eye, or a breath, but more accurately, as instantly as changing a channel on TV—it had happened so quickly that it wasn't harsh, not bitter. In fact, to the overheated dancers, the winter air was refreshing—as were their new dancing partners: fauns, some of them with umbrellas or bowler hats. Talking beavers and centaurs danced beside the middle-aged office workers.

"Scarecrow, this can't be right—"

"I know, I know, give me a moment, I've almost got it—"

The channel changed, and the air above them was filled with pre-teens on broomsticks, chasing a humming golden jawbreaker...

"Woops!"

The channel changed again, to a creepy drowned city under the sea. There were tentacles coming out of some of the buildings, and from the largest of them, there was a weird snoring sound...

"This is the worst one yet!"

"I know, I know, I'm all butterfingers today!" He punched a few more keys.

Then the channels flipped through several worlds in rapid succession:

—a flat, plate-shaped world on the back of four elephants, being swum through the galaxies on the back of a huge turtle…

"Darn darn darn darn darn!"

—under the sea again, this time with dancing clams and mermaids and a lobster singing calypso…

—an African jungle with singing animals and a baboon on a cliff holding up a baby lion cub…

"What are you doing?"

"I know, I know! It's stuck on the Disney Channel!"

"Well, do something!"

"Now I've got it!"

And as the Scarecrow typed, the street around them changed again. First it flushed a pale, timid little green, then a somewhat-less-bashful adolescent sort of chartreuse, and then finally, a confident, self-assured, cocky, almost obnoxious, shimmering, brilliant *emerald*…

And that's what Lyrissa Van Lear saw as she stormed out the main door of Perfection: a street that was now colored emerald green and filled with dancing people, of all kinds. *All* kinds. The dancers in the street had parted, leaving a narrow lane to the van in the center of the street. In front of the van, four figures were marching earnestly towards her. Lyrissa shuddered. The figures in the front of the van looked—familiar:

There was a Scarecrow, and a Patchwork Girl, easing on down the road towards her. And a broom—*her broom*—was bouncing cheerily along behind them. Beside them, a—shudder—little girl, *dressed just like her*, carrying a Macy's bag and wearing a backpack. Beside her was a young man in horn-rims—why did he look familiar? *And he was wearing her dress, too!*

And he looked better in it than she did.

They stopped at the foot of the steps of Perfection. Thunder rumbled and the sky darkened. Lyrissa Van Lear stood on the landing at the head of the steps, in her pink plastic crown and her fairy-princess dress with the bite out of it and the dirty brown train that had been dragged on the street. A wind rose, whirling around her.

"Nice dress," she purred. The little girl, obviously the one in charge, put down the shopping bag and tapped a pencil on the clipboard; the four of them grouped together. All movement on the street stopped; the dancers stood as silent and motionless as statues.

"How kind of you to visit me in my loneliness," said the witch. She sneered at Elizabeth and her companions, and her eyes stopped on the straw man. "I thought I'd seen the last of you." She took a green onyx cigarette lighter out of the handbag at her waist and looked at them for a moment. Then she lit it. "How about a little fire, Scarecrow?"

The flame became a fireball in her hand, and she lobbed it onto the Scarecrow. There was noise and confusion, as everyone leapt out of the way. But the

Scarecrow just stood there, arms folded, holding his ground. The flames danced over him, as if they were looking for a handhold and didn't know where to grab him; then they just sort of fizzled out, with an embarrassed, apologetic little fart. Elizabeth, Jervé and Scraps looked a little singed around the edges from the fire; but the straw man just stood there with an "is that the best you can do?" look on his face.

The Scarecrow said one word:

"Flameproofing."

Then one of the oddly dressed short people handed him a firehose. "How about a little water, witch?" and he twisted the nozzle and turned the firehose on, full blast. The water formed a corona around her, a fountain of white water in the shape of Lyrissa Van Lear. The four of them waited, expecting to see her dissolve into a puddle of witchy wickedness, but all they got was dampened in the splashback. When the hose was turned off, she still stood there, looking at them.

The witch said one word:

"Scotchguard."

Elizabeth handed the broom to Scraps and stepped forward. The witch flinched, shrank from the sight of what anyone could see was a Good Little Girl. But she put a brave face on it. "What do you want, little girl?"

Elizabeth was afraid. Any smart, sensible person would have been. But this was important. So she stood up straight, and managed to say without trembling, "Give me back my mother."

The witch smiled, cold and hard as stone. She

walked to the edge of the landing with a cool grace. She leaned down to Elizabeth and said quietly, "This world is mine. I don't have to give you anything, little girl."

She stood then, and turned to go back inside. Suddenly a troupe of yapping little white dogs tore out of the building, dragging their leashes behind them. They surrounded Lyrissa Van Lear in a noisy, toothy circle, yapping at her, jumping, and snapping at her heels. One of the dogs saw Elizabeth, and leapt off the platform into her arms, licking her face over and over again, whining and crying with joy.

Then, the dog in Elizabeth's arms turned to the rest of the dogs and barked a command. Immediately they circled the woman, a tight circle of growling little white dogs with sharp little teeth bared. Another command was barked, and each dog lifted his inside leg, the leg closest to Lyrissa Van Lear. The dog in Elizabeth's arms barked, clearly enough for anyone to understand, "Ready... aim..."

"Stop it!" The witch danced in the center of the circle, holding up her skirts, lifting one foot, then another out of firing range. She growled back at the dogs, "Do your worst, rodents. When I get inside, I'll make one phone call, and it's the dog pound for the lot of you." She kicked at the nearest dog, who yelped and scurried out of her way. She walked back to the edge of the platform, and said to Elizabeth, "You want your mother? Well, you've got her. You're holding her in your arms."

Then she raised her arms and called three times, a

word that sounded like a combination of baby birds being ripped apart by weasels and fingers being slammed in car doors. There was an answering screech from far above, and the sky filled with dots—tiny dots that grew and grew, coming closer and closer, until the air darkened above the crowd—darkened with *wings*. The witch clapped her hands in delight, hopping on tiptoe like an eight-year-old at a party.

The air above the street was filled with horrors. Filthy, grinning, shrieking nightmares crowded the sky above them, jostling impossibly, fanged and red-eyed, the air was filled with monkeys flapping on mangy, gnawed-looking wings. They looked down at the crowd below them, and gibbered, brown, broken claws outstretched, grinning, waiting only for the word, the signal, to attack. The crowd screamed.

"Please remain calm. There is no need to panic," the woman in the patchwork clown suit assured the crowd over a bullhorn. "Please distribute the Cha-cha Bags." The oddly dressed short people scurried around, handing out the brown-paper bags with "Cha-cha Bag" written in crayon on the side. The bags were handed, passed, and tossed—amazingly, there seemed to be enough to go around.

"Please open your Cha-cha Bag and place your hand inside." The street filled with rustling, as hundreds of bags were opened. All around the street, hundreds of dancers looked inside the bags and smiled.

The witch frowned. This was not the proper response—there was supposed to be terror, screaming, and fleeing for cover. Here, everyone stood waiting with their hands in little brown bags. And everyone looked—eager.

Enough of this! She whistled an ear-splitting whistle, pointing at the crowd. The flying monkeys' grins widened for a moment—this was going to be fun. They started their descent slowly, dropping, teeth bared, claws extended. The air above the street was filled with flying monkeys.

The patchwork lady with the bullhorn said, "Release the fruit!"

The air above the street was filled with flying bananas. People reached into their Cha-cha Bags, pulled out little bunches of two or three bananas, and threw them high into the air. The monkeys immediately forgot their attack, swooping and diving for the fruit, fighting in the air over bunches, and carrying them to cornices and ledges on the buildings high above the street, where they perched and ate. The only sound was monkeys eating, smacking their lips and crooning to themselves; that, and the splat of banana peels being dropped onto the street from a great height.

The crowd laughed. They laughed and pointed at the witch, as she stamped her feet in fury, shaking her fists and yelling obscenities at the monkeys. The monkeys ignored her and showered her with banana peels.

Her Perfect-Lady cool was completely gone now. Her hair was wild, blowing in the wind, her lipstick streaked across her face in a crimson smear, and she looked a little crazy.

"Ready to talk now?" asked Elizabeth, looking up at the witch.

The witch curled a lip. There was madness in her eyes. "Oh, yes," she said. "I'm ready to talk. Talk. Yes, we'll talk. But first let me change into something more comfortable."

She raised her arms and floated into the air, where she hung above the landing, looking down at Elizabeth. Then she began to turn, slowly at first, then faster and faster, spinning in the air above them and making a noise like a giant bee.

She blurred as she spun, her outline shifted as she spun in the air, her clothes whirled around her and expanded, growing larger and larger, and changing shape, filling the air above the platform with a huge darkness, too familiar: great, clawed haunches and an armored belly, black leather bat-wings flapping in the air, and a long, fanged lizard's head, smiling evilly, smoke curling from its nostrils. The dragon reared her head back and belched a stinking blast of fire into the air. She looked down at Elizabeth and smiled.

"Is that all you got?" said Elizabeth, bluffing madly. She was really glad she'd gone to the bathroom before she'd come.

"Why no, little girl, that's not all I've got. That's not all I've got at all." The dragon smiled, and then reared up like a great serpent, preparing to turn Elizabeth and her friends into crunchy bits of charcoal.

They huddled together, and the Scarecrow stepped in front of them and spread his arms. This was going to be bad, but maybe he could protect them for a moment—

The dragon vomited blue fire at them.

Suddenly, there was a blur in the air. The broom flew out from behind Scraps and was now in front of them, spinning in the air between them and the dragon. The broom spun so fast, it became a blur, then a solid blur, then a shield. The fire bounced off the shield, and Elizabeth and the Ozzites were protected and safe.

But as it whirled, the broom itself caught fire, and the whirling shield became, for a few moments, a magnificent disk of glorious blue flame. Then, the fire was over. A bit of ash was all that was left, drifting down, falling gently to the street like burnt newsprint. The broom was gone.

They all looked at the little pile of ash for a moment. Elizabeth didn't know how to feel, the broom had just—

"Serves you right," said the dragon, with a catch in her throat. "Traitor." She watched as the ashes, stirred by the breeze, lifted onto the air and floated up, away. "The world is full of brooms," she said. "There are lots of brooms in the world. I can always get…" She didn't finish, and her sentence trailed off into the silence.

"Enough. You've taken up enough of my time," she said, rearing up once more. "In another moment, this will all be over."

Elizabeth bent down and rooted in the Macy's bag on the ground beside her. She found the shoes at the bottom of the bag, and as the dragon inhaled, Elizabeth raised the shoes before her.

When the dragon saw the slippers, the silver slippers in Elizabeth's hands, she stopped, surprised. "Oh," she said.

"Yes," said Elizabeth.

"Oh," said the dragon. "Oh. My."

"Yes," said Elizabeth.

"You have?... well... in that case, perhaps we..." said the dragon.

"Yes?" said Elizabeth.

And the dragon looked out at the emerald-green street full of familiar characters, including her worker-bees and the Kyles, *none* of whom were coming in to work again, perhaps *ever*, and the monkeys who were still flipping banana peels at her, and she thought about... websites, and bank accounts, and... and the ashes of broomsticks.

Then she looked down at the Good Little Girl standing in front of her, holding her sister's shoes.

And the dragon sighed. "All right. We'll talk." In a blink, the dragon was gone. Lyrissa Van Lear stood before them now, looking tired, disheveled, and... silly, in her wild hair and plastic crown and ruined party dress. She looked at the shoes as if she was remembering something—remembering something that had made her happy once, remembering something that she'd lost.

"Truce?" said Elizabeth.

"What? Sure, whatever, truce. Come inside. Conference room's on the top floor." As the witch turned and walked into the building, her shoulders sagged. She looked old.

"Bring the shoes," she said.

They all went inside. The Oz folk, the Kyles, the little white dogs and many of the cha-cha dancers went up the stairs and into the Perfection building, following the little girl and the witch.

## CHAPTER THIRTY-FOUR

# The Elevator

It happened because there was so much confusion. The Oz folk were laughing and chatting and catching up on gossip, the Kyles were checking their hair in the stainless-steel of the Perfection lobby, the dogs were running around and sniffing things, and everyone was crowding to get onto the bank of elevators. Lions and tigers and sawhorses take up a lot of room in an elevator, not to mention middle-aged ladies in—"Excuse me! Excuse me! Watch your axe, Tin Man!"—really large bubbles. So there was a great deal of noise and confusion. Elizabeth walked on ahead, carrying her mom in the Macy's bag.

And that's how she ended up on an elevator by herself.

As the elevator doors closed behind her, Elizabeth collapsed against the wall. She'd been holding her breath for a long time. She'd done it. She'd done it! She turned around and whooped and jumped up and down and high-fived herself. She'd done it, everything had worked out, and at least for the moment, nobody was dead. Elizabeth looked down—her mother was snoring a little, sleeping peacefully in her bag. She always could sleep through a lot of noise. Elizabeth picked her up and hugged her, and her mom gave her face a sleepy lick. Gently Elizabeth set her on the floor next to the shopping bag.

Swanky elevator, she thought. Sea-green marble walls and floor, with veins of white whirling like sea foam. Tastefully indirect lighting, the climate perfectly controlled. Even the floor-number-button-thingies, sea-green lozenges on an onyx plate, were gorgeous. Persian kings' palaces probably weren't as nice as this elevator. It made Elizabeth feel small and sweaty. She moved away from the wall, not wanting to leave a smudge.

Elizabeth put her finger into her mouth. She really needed a good gnaw. Sorry, Mr. Lefty-Ring-Fingernail, it's been a bad week for you.

Elizabeth paused, mid-chomp. The elevator wasn't moving. She'd forgotten to press the button. Elizabeth reached out to push the button numbered "70"—

And the doors opened.

The Perfect Lady stood outside.

Lyrissa Van Lear nodded. "Little girl."

Elizabeth nodded back. "Witch."

"Mind if I join you?"

"It's your elevator."

"Not for long."

Huh? Elizabeth thought to herself.

"Do you mind if I ride up with you? The other elevators are full."

"No funny business."

"Of course not."

"Truce?"

"Truce, truce, I said truce, yes."

Elizabeth crowded her backpack, clipboard, bag and mother into the corner and made room for the Wicked Witch of the West.

The doors closed. Both of them hugged the walls. Elizabeth noticed that while her right shoulder pressed against the marble, Lyrissa Van Lear's left shoulder pressed just as hard on the other side. The chasm between them was full of pink dress. The two of them watched the numbers climb. 2 . . . 3 . . . 4 . . .

Slowly. This is really a slow elevator, Elizabeth thought, as she scratched at her neck, scratched at her waist, pulled the elastic waistband out, and kicked the skirt away from her ankles. The Perfect Lady pulled a compact out of her handbag and started trying to repair the damage. Smooth and push and pat the hair into place, a little concealer under the eyes, look, a little more, look, a little more... Elizabeth caught LVL checking her out in the mirror. Their eyes met. The Perfect Lady snapped the compact shut with a vicious *snap!* and jammed it into her handbag. Elizabeth smiled to herself. They both watched the numbers again. 23 . . . 24 . . . 25.

The Perfect Lady looked at her nails. She sighed and

crossed her arms. Elizabeth did, too. Each of them surreptitiously put a fingernail into her mouth and started to gnaw. Their eyes met again. Both of them stopped gnawing and watched the numbers again. 37... 38...

"You aren't going to change into anything awful again, are you?" said Elizabeth.

"I doubt it. Magic is hard work. Frankly, I'm bushed."

"Not exactly what people expect to hear from a witch."

The witch's eyes flashed a little. "You want to see a card trick? Shall I guess your weight?" Her eyes flicked to the numbers. "Magic is mostly about persuasion. I can do more with a thirty-second spot on the Super Bowl than I can with all the potions in the world."

"Or a website?"

"Websites can be useful, too."

"I always thought it'd be fun to be a witch."

"It has its perks. If you like warts."

They watched numbers. Elizabeth had an odd tingly sensation. She felt like she was alone in a dark, empty house, and that there was something growing in the corner, something dark and shadowy. And huge. With claws. She turned to look, and of course, there was nothing there, just the green marble walls of the elevator. But when she looked inside, in the corners of her mind, she found—a faceless, hulking shadow was growing there, getting hairier and toothier and nastier by the minute. It turned to look at her and—

"Stop it," she said to the witch.

The shadow evaporated. They looked at each other calmly.

"Persuasion."

"I see what you mean." Elizabeth reached into her backpack. "Chiclet?"

"No, thanks."

They watched numbers.

As they watched, Elizabeth thought to herself, very soothing in here. Soft music, indirect lighting, very tasteful. Calming. Relaxing. Soothing. She watched the numbers get larger and larger, 42, 43, 44, 49, 18, 19, 20, 20, 20, 20, 19, 17, 16, 23, 47, 18, 94—

"I said, <u>STOP IT</u>!" She reached into the bag and pulled out a squirt gun. "Don't make me use this."

"Scotchguard, I told you. I'm protected."

"Maybe. If this is water. Feel lucky?"

The witch frowned a little. "Okay, fine, whatever. Old habits."

The numbers started up again. Lyrissa Van Lear fished in her handbag. "Would it bother you if I smoke?"

"It's really bad for you."

"Nice of you to care."

Elizabeth noticed: As Lyrissa Van Lear put her lighter away, her hand trembled.

"Sorry about your workers."

"They'll be back in a few days, they all have mortgages. What was that song?"

"YMCA. People dance to it at weddings."

They watched numbers again for a while. "It's a silly dress, isn't it?" said Elizabeth.

"Hugely impractical. It's a dumb dress, really."

"And *uncomfortable*. Itchy, no pockets. You could never take it camping. Or on a hike."

"Probably not."

"Pretty though."

"Um-hm. Pretty."

They sighed, then watched the numbers some more. Then the Perfect Lady hit the red button and the elevator stopped. She turned to Elizabeth. "You can have it, all of it. I'll make you my heir. All this will be yours, and we can rule this world together—"

For a millisecond, Elizabeth was tempted. It might be fun to… Then beside her on the floor, her mother coughed, slightly. Elizabeth reached over and pulled the red button out. "No thanks." The elevator started again.

Numbers.

Then the Perfect Lady started to sniff. The sniffs turned to sniffles. Elizabeth looked at the numbers. Then she rolled her eyes. "I'm very intelligent, you know. If you think I'm going to fall for that, you're crazy."

But the sniffles didn't stop. When they became shuddery, sobbing gulps, Elizabeth reached out and hit the red button herself. The elevator stopped again. Elizabeth turned to look at Lyrissa Van Lear.

The witch had dissolved after all.

She was now sitting on the floor in the corner of the elevator, sobbing in a huge pile of dress. "Don't look at me," she said, turning her face to the wall, hiding her face with one perfectly manicured hand. "Stop looking at me, little girl. Stop looking at me. Please."

Elizabeth turned away. She tried to give the witch a little privacy, tried not to watch. She had never seen an adult cry, except for her mom at sad movies. This was not pretty at all. In the movies when people cry, it's one perfect tear trickling beside a trembling lip. In real life, there's snot.

Elizabeth crossed her arms. She thought she should be thinking, "Serves you right. Turning people's moms into dogs and stuff. That's terrible. Serves you right." That's what she thought she was supposed to be thinking. But somehow, it's not what was really going through her mind.

Elizabeth watched the woman sitting on the elevator floor sobbing and gasping, pounding the marble with one fist, noticing that she'd broken a nail, and wailing. This was becoming embarrassing. "C'mon, would you stop? Please stop," said Elizabeth.

Elizabeth opened up her backpack and took out a travel-size package of Kleenex. She offered it to the witch. The witch took the pack but couldn't even open it, she was crying so hard. She threw the package against the wall, then scrabbled to pick it up, and held it out to Elizabeth with a shaking hand. "Open it for me, please?" Elizabeth did and handed it back. The witch pulled out a handful of Kleenex, and held it against her eyes.

Elizabeth and her mother watched the witch cry. Elizabeth's mom walked over to the witch and sniffed at her for a minute. She barked once and did a little circle, standing on her back legs. It didn't help. Then the little white dog climbed up the enormous dress to the witch's hand, and started to lick it.

Elizabeth thought as she watched the witch. She remembered when she'd felt lost and hopeless, not so long ago; how awful it had been to feel so alone. She remembered how important little cotton hands had been to her; then, how much they had meant to her in that darkest time. Little cotton hands. Elizabeth thought some more.

Then she shoved the witch's dress out of the way and sat down on the floor beside her. Elizabeth put one arm around the witch's shoulders, and then the other one.

Elizabeth held the witch while she cried.

# CHAPTER THIRTY-FIVE

# Stories

The Perfect Lady didn't look perfect at all anymore: Her eyes were red and runny; her lipstick was smeared; tendrils of hair dangled around her face. "I never get—" She looked at the floor and breathed for a moment. When she looked up again, she just looked sad. "When is it _my_ turn? At the end, when this is over, you'll go down my hallway with all your little friends, taking everything in my life that's important. And I'll stay in my office with nothing in my hands, and as the elevator doors close behind you, I'll have to listen to all of you—" She hung her head a little, and the tears rolled down her face in a steady stream, "I'll have to listen to you… laugh."

Elizabeth patted her hand. "I promise, we won't laugh."

The witch smiled sadly at the floor. "You say that now. But you'll laugh, you'll see." She took back her hand and blew her nose. "You got a name, kid?"

"Elizabeth."

"Lyrissa."

"I know."

"Yes, you're very intelligent, you told me. I envy you, Elizabeth."

Elizabeth didn't know what to say. She picked up her mom and held her.

"Because a lot of people—it was clear out there, a great many people—*treasure* you. How important you are to them."

"You're important to a lot—"

The witch snorted. "Ha."

"People care about you."

The witch shook her head. "They suck up because they want something. Or because they're scared. They *love* you."

She looked at her hands, and picked at a chip in her green nail polish. "All my life—all my lives—I've always felt like I was outside, with my nose pressed against the window, and never a chance—"

The witch told her a story:

The little fat girl went down the stone steps into the cellar, into the cellar below the cellar. The air was warm and humid. Her face glistened. She'd worn her best dress, the new one, and her hard, shiny shoes, because Lucy and Elsie were waiting for her at the bottom, waiting for her, Lyrissa, and then they'd all be friends.

She held the lantern high, she hated the dark. But Lucy and Elsie were waiting at the bottom, and this was the last thing they'd asked her to do, and then she'd be friends with the prettiest girls in the school, and she'd be pretty, too. So she kept going down, and going down, and her breath got tight from the dark and the humidity, and she hoped she wouldn't get her asthma, but she wanted to be one of the pretty ones with Lucy and Elsie, so she kept going.

"Lucy? Elsie?" she called. She must be close to the bottom by now, and then they'd jump out and surprise her, and then they'd all laugh. Her words echoed on the hard stone walls, and her hard, shiny shoes slipped a little on the stairs, clopped the stone as she kept going down. She had her lucky shell in her pocket, and she rubbed it—it made her feel better, when she was afraid, or when she might be about to get her asthma, so she rubbed it.

She came to the bottom—the second subcellar, no one ever came down here, it was scary down here, and dark. She was really showing them what a good friend she'd be. She held up the lantern. "Lucy? Elsie? Where are you?"

It was a large room—what had they used it for? There were old wooden frames leaning against the wall, and piles of rusted metal. In the center of the floor was an old firepit.

"Lucy? Elsie?" They couldn't have forgotten, they'd talked about nothing else for two weeks, hushed, excited whispers. This had to be the right time, the right day, she'd written it down in her diary.

Maybe she was supposed to find something here

that would prove her to them, prove what a good friend she was. She started to look around.

Piles of iron, rusty and pointed, bars with handles, and ends like spears. The wood frames were big and heavy, crosses of wood, and there were iron rings in the arms of the crosses... and there was the pit—

No fire there now, of course, no fire for a long time. Lyrissa stepped to the edge, holding the lantern high—

Inside there was a package, with "Lyrissa" on the side!

It was pink paper, tied up pretty, with "Lyrissa" on the side!

She knelt to pull it out of the firepit. The knees of her new dress got dirty, but she didn't care, her hands shook with excitement, as she picked up the package—

The package had a weight, and something in it shifted in her hand—something wonderful, she was sure. Lyrissa shivered and closed her eyes, it was too delicious. She lifted one edge of the pink paper wrapping and slipped her hand in, to tease the shivery feeling out for as long as she could...

She felt something hairy and wet. She ripped the paper off.

Inside was a skinned rabbit from the kitchen, sharp nasty teeth and wet shiny muscle and milky dead eyes, glistening, awful, loosely blanketed with its own hairy skin.

Lyrissa threw it away from her, "Ugh! Ugh! Ugh," unable to scream, shaking her hands, holding them out from her, trying to get the slime off, wanting to wipe her hands on her dress, her one good dress, the new one she'd worn for this special— "Ugh!"

Then she heard them—Lucy and Elsie, hidden away above her, watching, watching her with her dirty hands, watching and giggling like mice, like two little mice, giggling at her, at her chubby red face, and the boiling hot tears that soaked her pretty blouse, giggling just like two little mice, two little giggling mice...

And she felt it then, true now, definitely true, forever and ever: not pretty. No. Not one of the pretty ones, not her, never Lyrissa—and her shame and embarrassment became a fireball in her tummy, a scalding ball of rage, of fury that choked up into her throat and blasted out of her mouth in a flame of words she'd never heard, words she didn't understand, and the mousy giggling became squeaks, squeaks just like two little mice; like *the two little mice, really, now,* that scurried now for cover, panicked and squeaking, scurrying in terror for a place to hide.

And Lyrissa, not good enough, never good enough, climbed the stairs to her room. As she passed the cowering mice, she stepped on them with her hard, shiny shoes, again and again, until the shoes were messy and red.

"Yow." Elizabeth watched the witch picking at the green nail polish on her perfect nails. She noticed that the nail of the witch's left ring finger was shorter than the rest, looked like it had been gnawed. "Intense."

"Yeah, you don't want to mess with a witch." Lyrissa

Van Lear blotted at her eyes and nose. "Even when she's eight years old. There's an old poem we always recited after stories:

> *The head, you'll learn, must rule the heart,*
> *Too soon old, too late schmart.*
> *But that was many lives ago;*
> *All of us learn,*
> *Some fast, some slow.'"*

"Did you really…?" said Elizabeth.

Lyrissa Van Lear looked at her with a blank, serious face that was impossible to read. "Why, no. Of course not. I was just embellishing. Lucy and Elsie turned up again in a few days, of course. They'd just run away. Of course.

"But, by then, it didn't matter. By then, they'd discovered I had Talent. When they found out you had Talent, they sent you off to study with the old women. Some girls went with the granny-types, who lived in cluttered houses with too many cats and helped deliver livestock and decide the colors of wedding dresses. Girls with more 'dramatic' Talent were shipped to the skinny old ladies who lived in castles in the mountains. Guess where they sent me."

Elizabeth and Lyrissa Van Lear were silent for a moment; for a moment nothing was said. Elizabeth just patted her mother, running her fingers through her mother's fur.

"Me, too," she said. "They make fun of me, too. 'Need some blunt-tipped scissors? Some markers, highlighters, stopwatch? Just ask Geek Squad.' They always come to me when their computers go down. But I don't get asked to the parties, either. Not the good ones. When I get to high school, I'll be valedictorian and editor of the class paper, and head of the Senior Prom Decorating Committee. And at the prom, I'll wear a nice dress, probably something like this one, and I'll serve the the punch. Because I won't have a date."

The witch patted her hand. "Sorry, kid. These next few years are probably going to be rough."

"Probably."

The two of them were quiet again for a moment.

"On our farm in Minnesota, there was a tulip tree, it's a kind of tree with leaves shaped like tulips? Well, every year, one morning in September I would come out of the house, and that tulip tree would be covered with butterflies. Really covered—every leaf had twenty or thirty butterflies on it, the whole tree was orange with this flock of monarch butterflies, on their way to Mexico. I'd get my mom, and the two of us would just sit in the grass and watch—remember?" Her mother barked softly. "Monarch butterflies. Thousands of them. Probably hundreds of thousands. They'd stop on our tulip tree to rest. "

The witch didn't move. She was as motionless and silent as a statue, listening.

"In the morning, when the sun hit the tree, it was like it was on fire. You could see the butterflies stretching their wings, moving a little, drying them out as they warmed in the sun. And then, as if there was a signal, they'd take off—first they fluttered around the tree, the tree would be hidden in this orange cloud of butterflies. And then they'd rise up into the air—mom said it was like a pillar of fire from the Bible—and they'd just ascend, rise up higher and higher until you couldn't see them anymore."

"I don't know why I thought of that just now. But it always gave me—I don't know, hope, I guess. Or something. These tiny little things—you know, they fly from Canada to Mexico twice a year?"

The witch looked at Elizabeth with an odd expression on her face.

"Yes, I did know that."

The two of them were quiet once more. Then Elizabeth continued, "But there's always…one or two, a couple of days before that, one or two flying on ahead, by themselves. Ahead."

"Um-hm."

"And I don't know, but maybe that's okay. Seeing things first, leading the way. Being… different. Maybe not everybody's supposed to be in a flock."

"Maybe."

They both sat thinking.

After a while, Elizabeth continued. "I mean, you definitely have… certain skills. Perhaps if you shared them in a slightly less… obnoxious way…"

"Um-hm," said the witch.

"Maybe things might work out a little differently."

"I get what you're saying," said the witch.

Elizabeth shrugged. "I mean… couldn't hurt to try."

The witch nodded.

Elizabeth reached into the Macy's bag. "Oh, and you should probably have these. They're yours." She pulled out the silver slippers and handed them to Lyrissa Van Lear.

The witch, surprised, held the shoes in her lap for a moment, and petted them like an old housecat.

"Is your power the greatest in Oz, now?" said Elizabeth.

"Not really. Mostly, all they're good for is going home. Home is where people love you. And there's no place..." she didn't bother to finish. "I'll probably just stay here."

She shook herself. "And how often can you wear silver slippers? They don't go with anything."

"Yeah, well." The elevator alarm bell rang. "We're missed," said Elizabeth. "They probably think you're doing something horrible to me. Um... you probably want to tidy up a bit."

"Thanks." Lyrissa Van Lear wiped her eyes again, and gave her nose a honk. She pulled out her compact and did what she could. "Damage control. How do I look?"

Elizabeth looked back at the witch for a moment. "Perfection," she said, with only a little irony.

"Yeah, right." Lyrissa Van Lear smiled a dry smile. "Well Elizabeth, shall we do this thing?"

"Might as well."

"Give me a hand. It's murder getting up from the floor in heels. Especially in this ridiculous dress."

It was a bit of a struggle, but together, they managed. Eventually, the two of them were on their feet.

"Ready?" said Elizabeth.

"Let's do it."

And they both reached, both hands went out to start the elevator at the same time.

CHAPTER THIRTY-SIX

# Partings

The elevator door opened to a circle of horrified, concerned faces. "Betsy, Betsy, are you all right?" said Scraps, as she and the Scarecrow tried to hustle Elizabeth away from the horrible, evil Lyrissa Van Lear. Elizabeth stopped them with a raised hand.

"I'm fine. Everything is going to be fine." Elizabeth turned to the witch. "Miss Van Lear?"

"Miss Callahan," said the witch.

Arm in arm, they walked into the conference room. The astonished Ozzites followed.

The conference room was full. Scraps, Oscar, the Scarecrow, a tin man, a lion, a man with a pumpkin-head, a spherical clockwork man, a sawhorse, a couch, several little white dogs, a large number of short people and a bossy middle-aged lady in a bubble, all jostled each other trying to make room. The middle-aged bubble lady seemed rather short-tempered, probably because several people in the room were wearing the same dress that she was.

"Well, dogs first, I suppose," said the witch, putting the shoes on the conference table and rolling up her sleeves. "Stand back, everyone, this can get a little messy."

A few minutes later, there was a popping sound like a large, oily bubble exploding: "bloit." Everyone looked at the bubble lady—"What? I'm fine!" But several young men in sharkskin got up, dusting their hands and knees with extremely confused looks on their faces.

Rose leaped to her feet. She ran to Elizabeth and swept her into her arms, crushing Elizabeth to her and crying *yi-yi-yi* yips. Elizabeth hugged her back, just as hard. And she cried a little, too. And she didn't care that anybody saw it. She wasn't embarrassed at all, not one bit. She was just glad.

The witch watched the reunion. "Don't worry—it takes a while to wear off. You may have to take her for walks for a few days."

The Oz folk folded their arms and got very stern-looking. They surrounded the witch in a large, multi-colored circle. The witch folded her arms and stood her ground, looking back at them. The middle-aged bubble lady floated against the ceiling of the conference room looking quite severe. She cleared her throat. She was obviously preparing to make a long, long speech.

Elizabeth raised her hand once more and stepped forward.

"It's under control."

"Excuse me?" the bubble lady sputtered. "Under

control?" She was disappointed—her speech was going to be a real wingdinger. "I don't know if we can believe that," she said, somewhat snootily. "We've heard that before."

Lyrissa Van Lear responded, "Oh, Glinda, why don't you take your enormous shiny bubble and shove it right up your enormous—"

"Like I said, I think things are under control," said Elizabeth. "Changes have been made. New leaves have been turned. I think from now on, things are going to be okay." She turned to the witch. "Won't they?"

"I suppose."

"Promise?" said Elizabeth seriously, taking the witch's hand.

The witch looked at Elizabeth. She looked at this Good Little Girl holding her hand and looking up at her, trusting her. The witch didn't understand why, but she felt her eyes tearing up. "Yes, Elizabeth, I promise," she choked out; for some reason, it was hard for her to speak. She laughed then, wiping her eyes. "Anybody got a Kleenex? I'm melting, I'm melting!"

Her joke just seemed to make everyone uncomfortable.

There was smattering of applause, and a couple of embarrassed coughs.

At first, the party was a lot of work. Everyone made the effort to let bygones be bygones. Lyrissa Van Lear made the effort to be a good sport, making sure that everyone had enough to eat, and mopping up spills with a paper towel. She and the bubble lady shared some frosty small talk: "Oh, fine, fine, time marches on, you know!" "Tell me about it."

But some of the Kyles had a little something hidden in a filing cabinet somewhere. Someone hooked up their iPod to the room's sound system, and there was some decent music, finally. Eventually, everyone started to loosen up.

And Elizabeth had never been so popular. People of all colors, shapes and sizes swirled around her. Everyone wanted to meet her, to praise her, to have their picture taken with her, to get her autograph. It was hilarious and chaotic and awesome and wonderful.

She wanted to stop time, freeze it for… forever. There were so many people she wanted to meet, wanted to talk to for a moment, wanted to get to know a tiny, tiny bit.

A man all made of tin made Elizabeth put her ear to his chest and listen to his heart tick, and he put a shiny funnel on her head—"Looks great on you! Keep it!" A lion as big as a horse bowed his head before her all the way to the ground like she was royalty, and gave her hand a terrifying sandpapery lick with a tongue the size of a dinner-plate. He insisted that Elizabeth get onto his back and hang on to his mane, and they spent half an hour racing up and down the hallways at full speed and laughing. Elizabeth shook hands with a giant bug in a top hat, and helped wind up a ball-shaped mechanical man in a derby. A sweet older man was a wiz at card tricks, and taught Elizabeth how to palm an ace.

Throughout all of this, Elizabeth watched the Perfect Lady out of the corner of her eye. Lyrissa Van Lear stayed on the fringes of the party, in the background, on the sidelines. Everyone made the effort to include her, but nobody talked to her for very long. She shared canning and preserving secrets with the man with the pumpkin head, who seemed to be very concerned about spoilage. She suggested a hairstyle change to a very unkempt man—"Have you tried hot rollers?"—and rust-control tips with the tin man. But mostly she seemed more comfortable being a little less social, staying a bit reserved and apart. As the party wound down, she had a long, quiet conversation with a gentleman dressed mostly in yellow. When she showed him the remnants of a broken pewter pin, he took the pieces and promised to repair it.

So all in all, for a party where everyone seemed to be trying to stay on their best behavior, it went about as well as it could. No accusations were made, no aspersions were cast (or spells), and everyone was cordial, at least.

Scraps tapped Elizabeth on the shoulder. "Well, our job here is done," she said. "We should probably be heading out now, little lady. Walk us to the elevator?"

Elizabeth stood for a moment with her mouth open. "What? You're going? Now? Can't you stay for a while? You haven't even met my—" she turned to introduce her mother, who was having her hand kissed by the Scarecrow.

"Charmed, I'm sure," said the straw man. "I can see where Elizabeth gets her beautiful, beautiful eyes…"

Scraps smacked him on the back of the head. "You are such a flirt," she said.

"Um, nice to meet you," said Rose. She found herself blushing and getting all girly. She had never been kissed by a scarecrow before.

"C'mon, Mr. Biology," said Scraps, dragging the Scarecrow into the hallway by a painted-on ear. Elizabeth and her mother followed. Around them, an amazing, noisy, colorful tsunami of Ozzites poured out of the conference room towards the elevators.

Then Elizabeth felt herself enfolded in a sweet, hay-smelling hug.

"Goodbye, my darling, we've got a tornado to catch," said the Scarecrow. "It's been delightful." Elizabeth crushed him in her arms. It was like hugging a huge pillow that smelled of summer, a huge pillow that hugged her back.

Elizabeth felt a stab in her foot. "Ow!" She looked down. "Ignore the bird," said Oscar, glaring up at her from the floor. "He's used to it. Don't bother saying a tender goodbye to the bird."

Elizabeth picked him up. She was surprised again at how heavy he was. The raven's black button-eyes looked into hers for a moment, then he said quietly in her ear, "Goodbye, broomstick-girl. You're going to have a very interesting life. Savor it." He flapped onto the Scarecrow's shoulder and they stepped onto the elevator.

Scraps stood at the side, waiting patiently for the last goodbye. Elizabeth turned to the Patchwork Girl. She looked up at the ridiculous clown-face smiling down

at her, and burst into tears, burying her face in Scraps' patchwork bosom. Scraps flopped her soft cotton arms around the little girl and hugged her back, petting the back of Elizabeth's head.

*"Betsy, Betsy, oh-so-fretsy,*
*Betsy's getting Scraps all wet-sy!"*

"I'll miss you," Elizabeth sobbed. "You're the best—the most interesting thing that ever happened to me."

"Oh, you say that now, Bets. But this is just the beginning of all the wonderful stuff that's going to happen to you—things that would never happen if you were dragging around a rag-doll girl and a scarecrow."

"I guess."

"Goodbye, Bets."

Elizabeth hugged her back. "This is… *really* hard," she cried.

"Yeah," said the Patchwork Girl.

*"Parting is such sweet sorrow,*
*That I could say goodbye till it be morrow."*

She scratched her head. "Did I just make that up? I'm *good.*"

Scraps knelt down, bringing Elizabeth's face close to hers. Her smile was a little sadder now. "You don't know it, but you've got a big heart, girlfriend," she said gently. "That's a good way to be. You'll be fine. Missing the people you love… just makes you love the ones you *have* a whole lot more." Scraps gave her one last hug, and stepped into the elevator beside the Scarecrow. She held his hand as she waved.

Elizabeth clutched her mother's hand and waved

back, as the elevator doors started to close. Then she let go of Rose's hand. "Hey Scraps, look! Funky Chicken!" And together Elizabeth and the Patchwork Girl of Oz solemnly did the Chicken Dance as the elevator doors closed.

Elizabeth watched the numbers above the door go down and down. She knew that when the doors of the elevators opened on the ground floor, the elevators would be empty.

But they would probably always smell a little bit of sweet, funny people. And magic.

Elizabeth turned around. In the conference room, Lyrissa Van Lear was leaning against the table. She'd been watching the farewells, alone, from a distance. She stood up. "Well, somebody should do some work today. This empire isn't going to run itself."

"Yeah. We should probably be going, too," said Elizabeth.

The witch looked down at her. "Will you visit?"

"Heck, yeah."

"Good. When?"

"How 'bout next Saturday? Have you seen the Museum of Science and Industry?"

"No, I haven't. But I'd like to."

"Good. We're on. It's a date." Elizabeth shook the witch's hand, then she walked with her mother to the elevator. Just before the doors closed, the witch said, "Wait a minute. You forgot these." She walked up to the elevator and handed Elizabeth the silver slippers.

"What?" said Elizabeth. "But, they're yours."

The witch nodded. "Why don't you keep them for me. They've been in your family for a long time. You might find them useful."

"Thanks." Elizabeth put the shoes into her backpack.

"One more thing—when I go online to check my bank account, will I have more than 'a measly two cents?'"

"Oh! Sure!" said Elizabeth. "Thanks for reminding me! I'll take care of it right away."

"Thanks. Appreciate it. Well, see you next week."

"See ya."

As the elevator doors started to close, the witch gathered her dress around her and started towards her office. Elizabeth reached out a hand and stopped the doors from closing. "Miss Van Lear?"

"Yes?"

"Did you notice? Nobody laughed."

The witch nodded, with a small smile.

The elevator doors closed.

Elizabeth turned to her mom. Rose looked down at her with her usual adoration, and Elizabeth was glad to see it. She squeezed her mom's hand.

"Nice to have you back, Mom."

"Rrrrrr-uff!"

"Wha—?"

"Just kidding. Nice to be back. I am so proud of you. You done good, pardner."

"Thanks. I did, didn't I?" Then Elizabeth gave her

mom an enormous hug. "It is _so, so_ nice to have you back. I missed you so much."

And Elizabeth and her mom hugged each other all the way down to the ground floor.

CHAPTER THIRTY-SEVEN

# The Scouring of the Shire, Or, A Little Fantastik Will Fix That Right Up

A new canine grooming parlor opened in a trendy near-north neighborhood a couple of months later. The upscale patrons, bringing in their Shih-Tzus and Shar-Peis for a trim, were very taken with the shop's owner:

"Isn't he wonderful? They call him, 'The Dog Whisperer!'"

"He's so good with dogs! It's like he's part dog himself!"

*Lincoln Bark*'s owner, Mr. Jervé, was an instant success.

"House to half... house out... warning on lights 3..."

In the back of the school cafetorium, Elizabeth was on headset in the darkened stage manager's booth.

Mrs. McCumber stood beside her, a mug of tea in her hands.

"Curtains, go... Lights 3, go!"

The darkened cafetorium was hushed for a moment. The curtains parted in darkness, and a single spotlight lit the stage. The music started, and the spotlight picked out a dancer. A male dancer. He stood in lavender tights, one hand poised over his head in a dramatic gesture. He was holding in his stomach and sticking out his chest, and he didn't look bad. Really. Ash didn't look half bad.

When the hoots and catcalls started, he didn't move. He was into it. He waited for the noise to die down. It did. Then he held out his hand...

"I can't believe you got him to do it," said Mrs. McCumber.

"It was surprisingly easy," said Elizabeth. "I can be very... persuasive. Go lights 4."

A second spotlight came up stage right, and into it stepped a little girl dressed in pink: pink tights, pink tutu, and a pink tiara glittering with pink sequins. She floated out on toe shoes, as if she was weightless, barely touching the ground. The crowd gasped a little. She was breathtaking. When she reached the center of the stage, she leaped into Ash's arms, and he lifted her over his head. Penelope hung there in the air, radiant and beautiful.

Elizabeth knew things were going to be all right.

"Go lights 5."

In the stage manager's booth, Elizabeth felt that she *belonged*, that she was in the *right place* —stopwatch in hand, calling cues that she'd carefully marked in her multicolor-tabbed, three-ringed promptbook covered with writing from many different extremely sharp colored pencils. "Lights 7... go."

Mrs. McCumber watched over her shoulder. "You know, you're good at this."

Elizabeth just nodded. She was busy. But she thought to herself, I am, aren't I?

Afterwards, Mrs. McCumber met the cast backstage. "That was wonderful! You all looked—so professional," she said, proudly.

"Thank you, Mrs. McCumber," said Penelope. "I was a little concerned on my entrance, I felt like the spotlight was lagging a tiny bit, and I was worried that the audience wouldn't get the *full impression* of the S.P.F.—after all, we had such a short rehearsal time, and I'd been feeling a little confused, but I knew, once I got into the light, everything would be fine..."

Even Ash, drying his face with a towel, blushed bright red when Mrs. McCumber complimented him. "The Talent Show was a huge success, people," she said. "Everybody into my car, I'm taking you all out for ice cream."

Elizabeth stopped packing her clipboard, stopwatch and promptbook into her backpack. "I'd love to, but I can't. I'm going into the city this evening. I'm meeting somebody. A friend and I are going to see a show."

The set looked very different now. Now, it could

only be described as... cozy. The stainless steel and the fluorescent lights were gone. Now, the set was a warm, welcoming caffé-latte brown, trimmed with pastel frosting colors. There were no sharp edges or corners anymore; now everything was rounded and comfy-looking.

One of the well-dressed young men turned to another and whispered, "Weird, isn't it?"

"The new set? Yeah."

"It's what She wanted."

"Does it remind you of anything?"

"Yeah, it does."

"Me, too."

"What...?"

"Gingerbread."

The studio door oiled open, and She swept in. The well-dressed young men gasped.

She was all in black—a full-length black dress with pumpkin sleeves and a cape. In her hand, she carried a black, wide-brimmed hat that came to a pronounced... point.

She put on the hat and whirled around. "How do I look, boys?"

"Um, well..."

"Isn't it a *scream?* Just right for the post-Halloween show, don't you think?"

"Um, yes, um, uh..."

"Oh, lighten up! You look like you've seen a ghost! Or a monster! Or... something." She winked at them. One of them dropped his clipboard.

"You boys need to loosen up. Is everything ready?"

"Yes, Miss Van Le—"

"Kyle, call me Lyrissa. And take some vitamins or something. Eat a sandwich. You look pale."

She swept onto the set and looked it over with a critical eye.

"Nice job. Looks very... homey. Well, shall we get started?"

"Um, Miss V—Lyrissa, there were some questions about the script—"

"Don't get your undershorts in a wringer, Kyle. I'm gonna wing it. I've got a couple of things to say."

She took her place behind the counter and looked at the camera. Kyle held up a hand. "Quiet, please. Rolling sound. And we're on in 5—4—3— — —"

"Good afternoon, and welcome to *Perfect Lady*, our post-Halloween show. I just wanted to talk to you for a moment about a couple of changes we're making."

"I've had a chance to do some thinking lately, and it seems to me life's pretty short. Too short, really, to worry about—" She sighed, "—this idea of 'perfection.' 'Perfection'—I mean, what the heck is it? You can spend your whole life chasing it, and never really..."

"Who has the time? I mean, there are books to read, and chocolates to eat, and..." and She looked directly into the camera, "—and new friends you'll want to spend some time with."

"So let's *let go* of that idea, shall we? It'll just make you nuts. And besides—" and she leaned in even closer, looking out at all her watchers, her face filling the screen, "—you're all just adorable, just the way you are."

"And <u>so am I</u>! So, today, we're doing a cute little craft project for Halloween, where we'll be gluing macaroni to a number 9 can of Campbell's baked beans, and spray-painting it gold. Won't that be fun?"

"Oh—and we're changing the title of the show. *Perfect* Lady just didn't seem right anymore. I thought about it a lot, thought of a lot of possible titles, things like *Close Enough, That'll Do, Looks Okay to Me.* But none of those seemed quite right. And then I had it!"

"So from now on, we're going to call the show, *Just Fine.* Now, where's that macaroni?"

# Epilogue

So, Alberta,

I was feeling so good—about myself, and
things, and you know, just, *life*—that a
friend and I went to see that show downtown
about us. I enjoyed the heck out of it! (But
just between us, a good deal of Artistic
License was taken...)

And afterwards, I went backstage and met the
cast. When they found out who I was, they all
wanted to take a picture with me! I felt like
a real celebrity!

I'm attaching the photo, here it is:

# The Hackers of Oz

And I went home with a nice new hat!

I think we both look positively *bewitching*, don't you?

xox,
Lyrissa

The
End

# ACKNOWLEDGEMENTS

So many people were hugely helpful in bringing this idea to fruition, and I'm thankful to all of them.

Shifra Werch, Stephanie Shaw, Kristine Thatcher, Kimberley Senior, Dale Calandra, Joe Foust, Carmen Roman, Tim Monsion, Goswami Kriyananda, and Greg Vinkler read early drafts and gave me hope, and some great observations and suggestions. Jody Stivers and Joanne Rosenbush gave superb proofing and editorial help. Tom Greensfelder and Marshelle Williams did their usual splendid work in putting the book together. Naama Friedman and Angela Iannone generously modeled for the final illustration. Len Rubin gave me sage advice and peace of mind.

The bulk of this book was written in Columbia College Chicago's Fiction Writing Program as my MFA Thesis. I had invaluable help and encouragement there from some wonderful teachers, among them Megan Stielstra, Joe Meno, Randy Albers, and Patricia Pinianski.

I would especially like to thank two people:

Jason Fuller, who, with his wonderful illustrations, brought my dreams to life, and lifted the book to a funnier, deeper, and richer level.

And Laurie Lawlor, who teaches several classes at CCC in writing for young people; without her help and encouragement, this book wouldn't be here.

# ABOUT THE CREATORS

AUTHOR Tom Mula has been an award-winning Chicago actor, director, and playwright for far, far, far too long. Audiences have tolerated his performances in a good deal of Shakespeare, as Koko in *Hot Mikado*, and in solo turns in *The Circus of Dr. Lao* and *Jacob Marley's Christmas Carol*. Tom also spent seven grueling seasons at the Goodman Theatre playing Scrooge.

Mula's plays include *Almighty Bob*, *The Golem*, Nicole Hollander's *Sylvia's Real Good Advice*, and adaptations of John Gardner's *In the Suicide Mountains* and *Dr. Jekyll and Mr. Hyde*. In 1995, Adams Media published Tom's book *Jacob Marley's Christmas Carol*; it was a *Chicago Tribune* bestseller. The award-winning play version has had hundreds of productions worldwide.

Tom spends most of his summers acting and directing at Peninsula Players in Door County, Wisconsin. He teaches in the Theatre Department at Columbia College Chicago. Tom Mula is a lucky, lucky man. He may be reached at tommula.com.


ILLUSTRATOR Jason Fuller is an illustrator and painter in Chicago, Illinois.

Through passionate observation of life influencing life, Jason strives to depict the magic of the world around him by giving unique visual representations of stories yet to be told.

"The most intriguing of images are captured in illustrations of the souls of living things interacting in a physical light."

www.jasonfullerillustration.com